PENGUIN  CLASSICS

THE CHIEFTAIN'S DAUGHTER

BANKIM CHANDRA CHATTOPADHYAY (1838–94) was the pre-eminent Bengali novelist of his day and is considered the father of the modern Indian novel. He was one of the first graduates of Calcutta University and had an extremely successful career as a district magistrate in the Indian Civil Service. He also wrote the country's national song, 'Bande Mataram'.

ARUNAVA SINHA translates classic, modern and contemporary Bengali fiction and non-fiction into English, and has thirty-four published translations to his credit. Twice the winner of the Crossword translation award, for Sankar's *Chowringhee* (2007) and Anita Agnihotri's *Seventeen* (2011), and the winner of the Muse India Translation Award for Buddhadeva Bose's *When the Time Is Right* (2013), he was also shortlisted for the Independent Foreign Fiction prize in 2009 for his translation of *Chowringhee*. Besides India, his translations have been published in the UK and the US in English, and in several European and Asian countries through further translation.

The Chieftain's Daughter

Bankim Chandra Chattopadhyay

Translated from the Bengali by
Arunava Sinha

PENGUIN BOOKS

PENGUIN BOOKS

USA | Canada | UK | Ireland | Australia
New Zealand | India | South Africa | China

Penguin Books is part of the Penguin Random House group of companies
whose addresses can be found at global.penguinrandomhouse.com

Penguin Random House India Pvt. Ltd
7th Floor, Infinity Tower C, DLF Cyber City,
Gurgaon 122 002, Haryana, India

Penguin
Random House
India

First published in Bengali as *Durgeshnandini* 1865
Published by Random House India 2010
Published in Penguin Books by Penguin Random House India 2016

English translation copyright © Arunava Sinha 2010
Introduction copyright © Shirshendu Chakrabarti 2010

10 9 8 7 6 5 4 3 2 1

ISBN 9780143425687

Typeset by SwaRadha Typesetting, New Delhi
Printed at Thomson Press India Ltd, New Delhi

www.penguinbooksindia.com

Contents

Introduction

BANKIM CHANDRA CHATTERJEE (1838–94) was one of the outstanding figures of that social and intellectual ferment often referred to as the Bengal Renaissance. His myriad-minded genius articulated itself with equal aplomb in fiction, satire, and essays on social, ethical, and religious problems. When he began editing the journal, *Bangadarshan* in 1872, it was hailed as an unprecedented cultural event. Its intellectual range, quality, and variety have never really been surpassed. Although he wrote his first novel, *Rajmohan's Wife* in English, he was obviously not satisfied and turned to writing fiction in Bengali. Between 1865 and 1869, he published his first three novels—*Durgeshnandini*, *Kapalkundala*, and *Mrinalini*—which occupied the margins of history and romance, realism and fantasy. With his fourth novel, *Bishabriksha*, he turned away from the remote to familiar social experience and its dilemmas.

However, despite its obvious affinity to romance, *Durgeshnandini* (1865) merits enjoyment and critical scrutiny as one of the earliest novels in India. No doubt, Peary Chand Mitra's *Alaler Gharer Dulal* was published earlier but it is more of a satirical sketch than a full-fledged novel. Apart from the fact that romance as a genre has not received the critical attention that has been given to the realistic novel, from the very beginning *Durgeshnandini* has not been considered as pure romance but as a blend of history and romance. As the historian Jadunath Sarkar has put it in the Bangiya Sahitya Parishat edition of Bankim's novels, many of the events and male characters are historically accurate while the women are products of the imagination; some events are historically incorrect because Bankim's source, one Alexander Dow, has been proved to be totally unreliable.

The historical background is the Mughal–Pathan conflict in eastern India at the time of Akbar. There is a reference to the same conflict in Bankim's second novel, *Kapalkundala* (1866) as well. In *Durgeshnandini*, Jagatsingh, son of Akbar's general Mansingh, is initially successful in containing Pathan insurgency in Bengal. When Fort Mandaran falls to the guile of the Pathans, its master, Virendrasingh, is executed and Jagatsingh is seriously wounded and imprisoned. Bimala, Virendrasingh's second wife, takes revenge by murdering Katlu Khan, the Pathan leader. On his deathbed, Khan offers truce and a treaty resolves the conflict. It is during these campaigns that Jagatsingh and Tilottama, Virendra's daughter, fall dramatically in love (in the very opening chapter of the novel) and Ayesha, Khan's daughter, is irresistibly drawn to the prisoner, Jagatsingh, while she nurses him back to health.

Durgeshnandini introduces Bankim's life-long pre-occupation with the role of overpowering passions in human life, often disruptive of settled and sober domesticity. Such emotional intensity can hardly be traced back to the English novel of that time, although comparisons have always been made with Walter Scott. A subtler but more pervasive Western influence on Bankim's fiction is perhaps that of Shakespeare. Bankim himself had argued in his essay on Bhavabhuti ('Uttarcharit') that there was not much room in Sanskrit aesthetics for accommodating the passions in their sudden and ungovernable fury, gripping us like passive victims in their clutches. In another essay, 'Shakuntala, Miranda and Desdemona', he compares the world of Kalidasa to the paradisial garden, but for Shakespeare the analogue he finds is that of the tempestuous sea.

Headlong, impetuous love is generated, and indeed heightened, against a backdrop of enmity and political upheaval. We may see prefigured here the link Tagore will explore between political turbulence and the release of erotic passion in *Ghare Baire* or *Char Adhyay*. *Durgeshnandini* contains the germ of the Romeo–Juliet story, in so far as the lovers are initially trapped in a long-standing family feud. Somewhat in the manner of Shakespeare, the uncertainty of the political conflict is transmitted to the urgency and intensity of love in the novel. Though courted patiently by the deserving Muslim nobleman Osman, Ayesha, the Pathan princess, hopelessly falls in love with the Hindu prince, Jagatsingh, arch-enemy and prisoner of her father Katlu Khan. These unforeseen happenings seem to take us from history to the realm of fantasy and wish-fulfilment. But the passions in Bankim's fiction play an emancipatory role, transporting the reader along with the characters to a visionary domain, that of the incalculable, removed from the obsequious colonial servitude that stifles the mind and spirit and which Bankim never failed to attack in his satirical sketches. There is perhaps a biographical urgency in all this. Being one of the two first graduates of Calcutta University, Bankim was promptly inducted into the colonial service and had to give up his legal studies. He considered this appointment as deputy magistrate and deputy collector a curse upon his life.

Even the story and the plot of *Durgeshnandini* is the consequence of a history of unbridled, though not emancipatory, lust: here the passions enslave and thereby take on the role of something akin to fate. Swami Abhiram had been a remarkably intelligent and studious scholar, but irresistibly drawn to the pleasures of the flesh. The illegitimate child born out of his sexual liaison with a local woman near Fort Mandaran was

Tilottama's mother. Exposed and humiliated, Abhiram exiled himself to Varanasi and pursued his studies further. But such was the ungovernable force of his sexual urge that a second liaison, this time with a low-caste woman, produced Bimala's mother. Again, what brings together the widower Virendrasingh and Bimala is reckless passion.

If the novel, in this description, seems to suggest a pot-pourri of sentimentalism, melodrama, and wild fantasy, it is more than redeemed by its poetry as also by a contrapuntal irony scaling down that poetry. Once again, we may recall Shakespeare who uses similar, contradictory, strategies to transform the sensational and sentimental crudity of his sources. Bankim's poetic language with its sinuous rhythm and sonorous power extracts the most it can from the inexhaustibly varied euphonic resources of Sanskrit. According to his younger brother, Purna Chandra, when Bankim, apprehensive of grammatical and stylistic errors, read out the manuscript to a select gathering, one of the pundits present declared that he had been so carried away by the language as not to notice any flaws; another asserted that the flaws had beautified the language further (*Bankim Prasanga*).

In historical terms, the novel marks the culmination of an attempt made by several learned authors and translators of Bankim's time to infuse the sinewy and resonant energy of Sanskrit into newly-emerging Bengali prose. Vidyasagar, the great social reformer, grammarian, and educationist, had not fully succeeded in this venture since his Sanskritized vocabulary was not entirely unburdened of erudition. Bankim's language, by contrast, is authentic Bengali and yet in its exalted register capable of opening up an order of reality for its readers far beyond the drab banality of Bengali social life in colonial times. Thus we enter on the wings of this language, a plane of intensity bordering upon the tragic. This can no longer be mistaken for the fake melodramatic strategies of sentimental romance.

As a counterpoint to the high poetic register we have a low register anchored in humdrum routine life involving, for example, soldiers' banter, maidservants' commonsensical chatter and above all, the farcical scenes centred on the clownish figure of Vidya Diggaj. The language used here is colloquial with an earthy, demotic tang that establishes a doubleness of style that is yet another of Bankim's achievements. Before him, the 'high' and the 'low' styles in Bengali had been kept apart: Kaliprasanna Sinha translated the Mahabharata into a heavily Sanskritized Bengali, but in his famous satirical sketch, *Hutom Pyanchar Naksha*, drew upon the lingo of the streets of Calcutta. In Bankim for the first time we have the two styles juxtaposed, resulting in a polyphonic fidelity to contemporary reality.

Since the oaf Vidya Diggaj imagines himself to be a latter-day Krishna hankered after by both Bimala and Aasmani (a maid servant), the reader must pause to question if the theme of love itself is not subjected to ironic scrutiny. The authorial voice of Bankim in *Durgeshnandini* already has a tongue-in-cheek undertone to its intimacy—this ironic detachment, carrying the suggestion of an alternative perspective, develops later into an integral part of his novelistic art. The intensity and mood of total surrender in the love of Ayesha, Tilottama, Jagatsingh, and Bimala is travestied not only by these farcical episodes but also by the constant reminder of women as war booty, an object of the insatiable sexual appetite of the power-hungry male.

If the power of women is displayed in their ability to use their charm—Bimala, for instance, mesmerizes her guard as well as Khan himself—a much higher power is suggested in Bankim's intoxicated but intellectually controlled description of female beauty. We must not forget that women were largely confined and concealed within the inner quarters of the household. Bankim makes them confidently visible, each woman's beauty distinct from that of the other. As readers we are impelled to admire the beauty of Tilottama, Ayesha, and Bimala not furtively or guiltily; the poetry is thus once again emancipatory, inspiring us to uninhibited enjoyment and admiration. At the same time, in keeping with the farcical interlude involving Vidya Diggaj, this exalted poetry with its Sanskritized vocabulary and interlinked compounds is exactly mimicked in the description of Aasmani's beauty but now in an unmistakably parodic vein.

Despite the elaborate description, the women are not rendered objects of male fantasy and desire; rather, their beauty is inseparable from their selfhood, identity, and even agency. It is a picture, the best picture, of a woman's inner vitality, reinforced by constant association with nature in her regenerative and elemental potency. In fact, nature lends a contemplative dimension to the novel. Much of the significant action takes place in darkness when the familiar visible world melts away and silhouettes and reflections in water take over. By contrast, Katlu Khan's depraved pleasures of the harem are accompanied by the hard glint of concubines' ornaments in artificial light.

It is natural vitality that expresses itself in the women's passions which drive them beyond the usual social bounds and conventions. Overpowered by passions—at a moment of dramatic crisis, Tilottama, the youngest and most vulnerable, faints and falls ill—the women nevertheless manage more than the men to keep their emotional turmoil in control. Tilottama responds to a contrite Jagatsingh without any bitterness or resentment and Bimala reconciles herself happily to the undignified secrecy of her marriage. But the best example of this self-control is of course Ayesha who is in many ways the central figure of the novel. The fire of love burns within her silently and imperishably, expressing itself in a rare generosity of spirit and strength of character. Stung by her unsuccessful and jealous suitor Osman's accusations, she declares her love for Jagatsingh with a bold candour that marks the culmination of the empowerment of women.

Both Tilottama and Ayesha, the two heroines, vastly different as they are, are characterized by an openness of nature that contrasts oddly with the guile and duplicity to which women would have been habituated because of their social situation. Bimala reminds Jagatsingh that a woman is compelled by society to lead a hidden life and cannot reveal her identity. Of course, Bimala knows how to manipulate people, especially men, but she remains steadfast in her passionate loyalty to Virendrasingh. If contemporary social conditions do not offer models for Bankim's women (as they do not for Shakespeare's women as well), they are not creations of wish-fulfilment either; rather, they embody the tendencies and possibilities latent in their world. It is for this reason that the women are shown in situations of solitude and reflection; both Bimala and Ayesha communicate their feelings and experiences in the introspective form of the letter. After meeting Jagatsingh, Tilottama is shown at twilight in a mood of reverie at a window, contemplating her mind, as it were, in the eddies of river Amodar flowing by the fort. At the end of the novel, Ayesha is similarly situated late at night by a window, observing her mental state in the moat brimming over with water quietly reflecting the starlit sky.

Shirshendu Chakrabarti is Professor of English at Delhi University and a published poet and critic in Bengali.

Part One

Chapter One

The Temple

AT THE END of summer in the Bengali year 997*, a solitary individual was travelling on horseback from Bishnupur to Mandaran. Observing the sun preparing for its decline to the west, the horseman spurred his steed into a faster gallop. An enormous expanse of land stretched out before him; who knew, if a violent thunderstorm were to strike in the twilight, crossing the terrain would then prove considerably difficult, for it offered no shelter. No sooner had he traversed that vast stretch of land than the sun set; indigo clouds gradually enveloped the night sky. So impenetrable was the darkness that shrouded the horizon that riding appeared hazardous. The traveller stumbled along, the road only occasionally illuminated by flashes of lightning.

Presently, the summer thunderstorm broke with a deafening roar, accompanied by torrential rain. Losing his bearings, the man on horseback no longer knew which way his destination lay. Slackening the reins, he allowed his horse to proceed at will. After they had travelled aimlessly for some time, the stallion lost its footing when its hoof encountered a solid object. A flash of lightning at that instant provided the traveller a momentary glimpse of a large white structure. The horseman leapt to the ground surmising that it was a building. He realized immediately that his mount had

---

*1592 Common Era.

missed its footing on impact with the stone staircase of the edifice. Aware that shelter was close at hand, he released his horse and stepped carefully on the flight of stairs. Another flash of lightning revealed that the building before him was a temple. Skillfully negotiating his way to its small entrance, he found the door barred; feeling his way about with his hand, he concluded that it had been locked from within. The traveller wondered curiously who at this hour could possibly have locked the door of a temple in such a remote area. But with the rain assaulting him furiously, it did not matter who was within. The man hammered on the door with all his strength, but no one appeared to open it for him. His inclination was to kick the shutters open, but he desisted from going to such lengths lest this imply sacrilege towards the gods. Eventually the timber panels, unable to withstand his mighty blows for long, were praised loose. As soon as he entered the interiors of the temple, the young man heard a muffled cry. Almost immediately the lamp that had been flickering faintly went out with the entry of the storm. The entrant could see neither the humans nor the idol of the god within. Aware of his predicament, the intrepid youth only smiled wryly, and then bowed reverentially in greeting to the invisible deity in the sanctum. Rising, he called out in the darkness, 'Is there anyone in here?' No one answered, but he heard the jangle of ornaments. Concluding that it was unnecessary to waste words further, he reinstated the door in its original position to keep the storm at bay and, placing his own body against the breach, repeated, 'Pay attention, whoever you may be, I am fully armed and have stationed myself by the door. Do not interrupt my repose. If you dare, and are a man, you shall face the consequences; if a woman, go to sleep in peace, for as long as a Rajput retains his sword and buckler, not even a blade of grass can pierce your feet.'

4

'Who are you?' a feminine voice asked from somewhere within the temple.

'From your voice I gather that it is a lady who wishes to know,' answered the traveller in surprise. 'How will it benefit you to know who I am?'

'We are frightened,' came the response from the heart of the shrine.

'No matter who I am,' replied the youth, 'it is not our custom to reveal our identity to maidens. But ladies need fear no harm while I am in their presence.'

'Your words fortify us,' answered the woman. 'We were all but dead with fear all this while. My companion is still faint. We had arrived here at dusk for the ceremonial worship of Lord Shiva. Afterwards, when the storm descended upon us, our maids and servants abandoned us and vanished we know not where.'

'Pray do not worry,' the young man assured them, 'rest now. I shall personally escort you home at daybreak tomorrow.'

'May the Lord protect you,' responded the woman.

The night had half elapsed, the rainstorm abated, whereupon the youth said, 'Please be bold enough to wait here by yourselves awhile. I shall visit the village nearby to procure a lamp.'

At this, the woman said, 'There is no need to go as far afield as the village, sir. The guard of this temple lives close at hand; the moon is out, you will see his cottage as soon as you step outside. He always has a stock of lamps in his home'. At her bidding, the young man stepped out and found the temple guard's dwelling by the moonlight. Arriving at the entrance of his house, he awoke the owner, who was too fearful to open the door. The guard observed the intruder from the confines of his home and when close inspection did not yield any signs of the visitor being a bandit, and the lure of lucre in particular proved impossible to resist, he opened the door and lit a lamp.

Returning with the lamp, the traveller now saw a white marble idol of the god Shiva in the centre of the temple. Two solitary women were visible behind the idol. The moment she saw the light, the younger of the two bowed her head, drawing a veil over her face. On observing the diamond-studded bracelet around her bare forearm, her intricately embroidered attire enhanced with jewels as well as royal patterns and motifs, the traveller felt certain that this young woman belonged to no ordinary lineage. From the relative lack of embellishments in the other woman's garments, he surmised that she served as a companion and maid to the younger woman, although more accomplished than maids usually are. She appeared to be approximately thirty-five years of age. It was not difficult to realize that his conversation had been conducted with the older of the two women. He also noted with surprise that neither of them was dressed like women of the region—both were attired like ladies from the west, that is, not from Bengal but from greater Hindustan. Placing the lamp at a convenient spot, the youth approached them. When the light played over his figure, the women realized that the stranger could only be a little older than twenty-five. His physical stature might have seemed disproportionate on another person; but he was so broad of chest and his body so well sculpted that his height in fact added a divine comeliness to his appearance. His tender charm was as appealing as—or even more than—that of green shoots newly born after the rains; his armour was of the hue of young leaves of spring, his sword was slung in its sheath from the girdle at his waist, and he held a long spear. On his head was a turban, with a solitary diamond on it; from his ears dangled pearl earrings; a bejewelled amulet hung around his throat.

At first glance, both the women and the man felt desirous of learning one another's identities, but none wished to be uncivil enough to be the first to enquire.

Chapter Two

Conversation

THE YOUNG MAN was the first to express his curiosity. Addressing the older of the two women, he said, 'I sense that both of you are ladies from families favoured by fortune, I am hesitant to ask who you are; but perhaps you do not share my constraints when it comes to revealing your identity, which is why I am emboldened sufficiently to enquire.'

'What, for that matter, is a woman's identity?' the older one answered. 'How should they who are unable to assume their family title identify themselves? How can those who are compelled to live secret lives ever reveal themselves? When the Lord forbade women from uttering their husbands' names, He also robbed them of their own identities.'

The young man did not respond, for he was distracted. Still concealed behind her companion, the younger of the two women had slowly lowered her veil to gaze steadfastly at him. During their conversation, the traveller's eyes turned in her direction; they could not turn back. He felt that he would never again behold such a miraculously beautiful woman. The young woman's eyes met the young man's. She lowered hers at once. Not receiving a reply, the companion looked at the traveller. Following his eyes, and realizing that the woman accompanying her was also staring at the young man fervently, she whispered in her ear, 'Well? Are you planning to select your own husband in the presence of the Lord?'

Pressing her companion's hand, the younger woman spoke just as softly, 'Go to hell.' This girl in my care appears likely to fall prey to the love god's arrow at the sight of the spiritedly handsome stranger, mused the shrewd attendant. Whatever else might ensue, she worried, her peace of mind will be destroyed forever. Such an eventuality had to be prevented immediately. But how was she to succeed in this endeavour? Concluding that it was her duty to dispatch the young man elsewhere through suggestion or guile, she said with feminine cunning, 'Sir! A woman's good name is so fragile that it cannot even withstand the wind. Surviving this terrible storm tonight had seemed well-nigh impossible, but since it has stopped now, let us see if we can go back.'

'If you must leave at this hour of the night,' answered the young man, 'I shall escort you personally. Since the skies have cleared, I would have left for my destination by now, but I cannot depart without ensuring protection for someone as beautiful as your friend.'

'Sir, we are unable to disclose everything lest you consider us ungrateful for the kindness you have extended to us,' responded the woman. 'What can we possibly tell you about the ill fate that befalls women? We are easily mistrustful; it will be our good fortune to have you escort us home, but when my master—this lady's father—asks, who accompanied you on this night, what answer will she provide?'

After a few moments' thought, the young man said, 'She may state that she was accompanied by King Mansingh's son, Jagatsingh.'

The women could not have been more startled by a clap of lightning within the temple. Both of them were on their feet instantly. The younger one retreated behind the stone representing Shiva. The older one, so adept at conversation, draped the end of her saree around her neck. Prostrating

8

herself, she said, 'Your Highness! We have offended you a thousand times out of ignorance; pray permit your generosity to forgive us dim-witted women.'

'There can be no forgiveness for such a grave offence,' the young man said smiling. 'But I shall forgive you if you tell me who you are, or else you shall receive fitting punishment.'

Gentle words always make the discerning woman courageous. The lady said with a smile, 'What is the punishment, we are ready.'

Also smiling, Jagatsingh said, 'That I shall escort both of you home.'

The companion realized that severe danger lay ahead. She was unwilling to reveal the identity of the younger woman to the general of the Emperor of Delhi's army; if he were to escort them back, it would cause greater damage, for it would amount to much more than disclosure. She continued to look at the floor.

At that moment the drumbeat of hoofs was heard not far from the temple; anxiously emerging outside, the prince observed a group of nearly one hundred horsemen riding by. A single glance at their uniform revealed that they were his Rajput soldiers. The prince had earlier visited the Bishnupur area on war-related business, and had been on his way to meet his father, accompanied by one hundred members of the cavalry. In the afternoon he had left his retinue behind; but because they had all taken different routes, he had run into the thunderstorm all by himself. Now he attempted to find out whether his soldiers had seen him, crying out loudly, 'Long live the Emperor of Delhi.' At once one of the horsemen approached him. 'I was waiting here because of the thunderstorm, Dharmasingh,' the prince told him.

Bowing, Dharmasingh said, 'We have been searching everywhere for Your Highness, we have brought your horse —we discovered him near that banyan tree over there.'

'Wait here with the horse,' Jagatsingh instructed. 'Send two people to fetch a palanquin and accompanying bearers, tell the rest of the soldiers to advance.'

Dharmasingh was somewhat surprised by these instructions, but knowing that it was incorrect to question his commander, he simply said, 'As you please, sir,' and proceeded to convey the prince's instructions to the troops. When told about the palanquins, some of the soldiers smiled wryly at one another, saying, 'A novel strategy today.' 'And why not?' another remarked. 'The royals have hundreds of consorts, after all.'

Meanwhile, taking the opportunity of the prince's absence, the beautiful young woman removed her veil and asked her companion, 'Why are you unwilling to reveal our identity to the prince, Bimala?'

'I will answer that question to your father,' responded Bimala. 'But what is this uproar I hear again outside?'

'I imagine the prince's troops must have been looking for him,' answered the young woman. 'Surely there is nothing to worry about while the prince is here?'

Before the horsemen who had departed in search of palanquin-bearers could return, the bearers and guards who had deposited the women inside the temple and taken shelter from the storm in the nearby village came back. Spotting them from a distance, Jagatsingh re-entered the temple to tell the older woman, 'Some armed people are approaching with a palanquin and bearers, can you come outside to identify whether they are your people?' Standing at the door, Bimala confirmed that they were.

'Then I shall not tarry here any more,' said the prince. 'A confrontation might cause harm. I am leaving but I pray to the lord that you reach home safely. I request you not to reveal before a week has elapsed that you met me here; do not forget our meeting, however. Please accept a small token in

10

remembrance of our encounter. As for me, that I did not learn the identity of the daughter of your master shall remain as a keepsake in my heart.' Extracting a pearl necklace from his bejewelled turban he placed it on Bimala's head. Weaving the valuable ornament into her hair, Bimala bowed deferentially to the prince, saying, 'Please do not hold it against me for not disclosing our identities. There is a very good reason for it. If indeed you are assailed by extreme curiosity, tell me where to meet you a fortnight from today.'

After some thought Jagatsingh said, 'A fortnight from today, you can meet me here at this same temple at night. If you do not see me here, it means we shall never ever meet again.'

'May the gods protect you,' said Bimala, bowing again. After another irascibly yearning glance at the young woman, the prince leapt on to his horse and disappeared.

Chapter Three

Mughals and Pathans

JAGATSINGH BEGAN HIS journey from the temple of Shiva at night. For the moment I am unable to satisfy the gentle reader's curiosity by pursuing him on his way or by providing information about the enchantress within the temple. In order to explain why the Rajput Jagatsingh was visiting Bengal or why, indeed, he was travelling alone through that open stretch of land, it is necessary to briefly describe certain political events of that era in Bengal. Impatient readers may abandon these accounts, but the author's opinion is that impatience is not advisable.

After Bakhtiyar Khilji established Muhammadan rule by conquering Bengal, Muslim kings ruled the state unopposed for several centuries. In the Islamic year 972*, the renowned sultan Babar defeated Ibrahim Lodi, the Emperor of Delhi, in a battle for the throne; but Bengal did not come under the rule of the descendants of Timur Lang immediately.

Before Akbar's reign, which marked the pinnacle of the Mughal dynasty, Bengal had been ruled by independent Pathan kings. In an ill-advised move, the foolish Daud Khan trod on the sleeping lion's tail; as a consequence he was defeated by Akbar's general Monaim Khan and dethroned. In 982, Daud fled to Utkal** with his retinue; Bengal was annexed

---

*1564 Common Era.
**Orissa.

by the Mughal empire. But after the Pathans had established themselves in Utkal, the Mughals found it difficult to uproot them. In 986, however, Khan Jahan Khan, representative of the Emperor of Delhi, defeated the Pathans for the second time and brought the Utkal kingdom under the rule of his master. But this victory was followed by yet another uprising. The new system of tax collection instituted by Akbar Shah made all landowners bristle with dissatisfaction. Each of them took up arms to protect their authority over their respective realms. With a violent revolt brewing against the emperor, Utkal's Pathans reared their heads once again, and, establishing one of their own—named Katlu Khan—as their ruler, proclaimed independent status for their state. Midnapore was also added to their kingdom.

Neither the competent royal representative Khan Azeem, nor Shahbaz Khan after him, succeeded in wresting the lost kingdom back from the hands of the enemy. Eventually a Hindu warrior was dispatched to accomplish this difficult feat.

Intelligent as well as wise, Akbar was far more astute in every respect than his predecessors. He had developed the conviction that native affairs of a state were best conducted by natives—that foreigners could not perform them as competently. He believed, too, that in their aptitude for war or for administration, the Rajputs were head and shoulders above the rest. Thus he always appointed native Indians, specifically Rajputs, for important administrative tasks.

Among the Rajputs who held high positions at the time of these events, was Mansingh. He was the brother of none other than Akbar's son Salim's wife. When Azim Khan and Shahbaz Khan both proved unequal to the task of conquering Utkal, Akbar installed this illustrious figure as governor of Bengal and Bihar.

Arriving in the city of Patna in 996, Mansingh first quelled all the other small rebellions. Desirous of victory in Utkal, he departed for that region the following year. With the intention of establishing his residence in Patna, he had appointed Syed Khan his representative for ruling Bengal. Entrusted with this responsibility, Syed Khan was stationed in the city of Tanda, the capital of Bengal at the time. Venturing forth in anticipation of more battles, Mansingh invited his representative to join him. He wrote to Syed Khan, informing him that he wanted to meet him with his troops at Bardhaman.

Arriving at Bardhaman, however, the king discovered that Syed Khan had not arrived. He had only sent a message through a herald, to the effect that he was likely to be considerably delayed amassing troops; in fact, the monsoon would be upon them before he could prepare his army. Therefore, if King Mansingh would deign to maintain his camp at Bardhaman, occupying it till the end of the monsoon, Syed Khan would appear in his royal presence, accompanied by his soldiers. Accepting this suggestion since he was left with no alternative, King Mansingh established camp by the Darukeshwar river and proceeded to wait for Syed Khan.

During his sojourn there, the king was informed by messengers that his inactivity had emboldened Katlu Khan to approach Mandaran with his troops in order to plunder and pillage. Worried, the king decided it was necessary to dispatch one of his senior generals to investigate the location of the enemy, their motives, their activities, and so on. His favourite son Jagatsingh had accompanied Mansingh to battle. Learning of his eagerness to perform this daring act, the king sent him towards the enemy ranks, accompanied by a hundred members of his cavalry. Accomplishing his task swiftly, the prince was on his way back. The esteemed reader has already been acquainted with him during his return to his own camp.

Chapter Four

The Young General

WHEN JAGATSINGH ARRIVED at his father's camp after leaving the temple, King Mansingh learnt from his son that nearly fifty thousand Pathan soldiers had set up camp near the village of Dharpur and were plundering the villages, more or less unhindered, having constructed or occupied fortresses in several places. Mansingh realized that the villainous Pathans had to be subjugated immediately, but also that it would prove to be an arduous task. Summoning all his accompanying generals to determine the course of action, he said, 'Every passing day one more village, one more district is slipping out the hands of the Emperor of Delhi. These Pathans must be made to submit at once, but how will that be possible? They are more numerous in strength than we are; moreover, they have built fortifications to protect themselves. Even if we were to defeat them in battle, we will not succeed in annihilating or even displacing them; they will survive easily within their fortresses. But consider, were we to be defeated on the battlefield, we would have no protection from the enemy, who would certainly slaughter us. Such foolhardiness will mean much damage to the Emperor of Delhi's army, destroying all hope of conquering Orissa. It would be politic to await Syed Khan's arrival with reinforcements. On the other hand, the enemy must be brought under our control with utmost urgency. What is your counsel, gentlemen?'

The experienced generals advised in unison that for now, it was their duty to await the arrival of Syed Khan. 'I intend not to risk the obliteration of our entire army, but to dispatch a small number of soldiers under an able general to engage with the enemy,' declared King Mansingh.

'Your Highness! When we fear to send large contingents of our soldiers, what can a small number possibly accomplish?' enquired an experienced Mughal general.

'I do not wish to send a small force into open battle,' answered Mansingh. 'However, remaining under cover will enable it to overcome some of the Pathan groups engaged in tormenting villagers.'

'Which of your generals will willingly walk into the mouth of inevitable death, Your Highness?' countered the Mughal general.

Frowning, Mansingh enquired, 'Do you mean to say there is not one among so many Rajput and Mughal military leaders who does not fear death?'

Six or seven Mughals and Rajputs rose at once, each stating, 'Your servant is ready, Your Highness.' Jagatsingh was present too; he was the youngest among the gathering. Standing behind the rest, he said, 'With your permission, this servant would also like to participate in achieving the Emperor of Delhi's objectives.'

Smiling, Mansingh said, 'And why should it not be so? Today I am convinced once more that the extinction of Mughal and Rajput glory is not imminent. Since all of you are ready for this challenge, whom should I choose for the mission?'

'Your Highness! How splendid it is that there are so many volunteers,' said one of the councillors with a smile. 'You can use the opportunity to expend as few soldiers as possible. Place the responsibility for the royal mission on the one who requires the fewest warriors to accompany him.'

'Excellent suggestion,' said the king. 'How many soldiers do you wish to take with you?' he asked the first volunteer. 'I shall perform the emperor's bidding with fifteen thousand foot-soldiers,' the general responded.

'If you were to carve out a contingent of fifteen thousand soldiers from this camp, not many would be left. Which of you intrepid generals is willing to fight with ten thousand?'

The generals were silent. Eventually a favorite of the king, the Rajput warrior Yashwantsingh, sought permission to fulfil the royal edict. The king cast pleased glances upon everyone present. Prince Jagatsingh had been waiting to catch his eye—as soon as the king's glance alighted on him he said deferentially, 'If it pleases Your Highness, your servant will require the assistance of only five thousand soldiers to deposit Katlu Khan on the other bank of the Subarnarekha.'

King Mansingh was astonished. His generals began to whisper amongst themselves. After a few moments the king said, 'My son! I am aware that you are the glory of the Rajput clan, but you are being foolhardy.'

'If I cannot keep my word and squander the sovereign's soldiers, I shall be guilty of violating the king's law.'

After a few moments' thought, Mansingh said, 'I will not come in the way of your adhering the code of the Rajput; I select you for this mission.'

After enfolding the prince in an emotional embrace, the king departed. The generals returned to their respective window.

Chapter Five

Fort Mandaran

SIGNS STILL REMAIN of the path along which Jagatsingh had returned to Jahanabad from the province of Bishnupur. The village of Mandaran was a little to its south. It is an insignificant hamlet today, but at that time it was a city of splendour. It was this city that the ladies whom Jagatsingh had met in the temple departed for after he had left.

Mandaran was known as Fort Mandaran, possibly because it contained a few ancient forts. The Amodar river flowed through the city; at one point its course had curved sharply, surrounding a triangular tract of land on two sides, whilst on the third side there was a sunken fort. At the spot, where the river began its arc, a gigantic fort rose from the level of the water to the sky. Built from base to spires in black stone, it rested on foundations that were battered from both sides by powerful river currents. Even today visitors to Fort Mandaran can see the sprawling ruins of this once-impregnable fort; only the base remains now, the rest of the structure has been ground to dust by ravaging time. The ground is covered by a dense forest of tamarind and myrtle trees, with their attendant vines and tendrils, sheltering snakes, bears, and similar ferocious beasts. Earlier there had been more forts on the other side of the river.

The fort was built by Ismail Ghazi, the famous general to Hosen Shah, the most illustrious of the Pathan kings of Bengal. But subsequently, it became the fiefdom of a Hindu warrior named Jaidharsingh. At the time of our story, his descendant Virendrasingh lived there.

In his youth there was no love lost between Virendrasingh and his father. Being arrogant and reckless by nature, he seldom followed his father's instructions, the result being constant squabbles and arguments between father and son. The aged landowner arranged his son's marriage to the daughter of another landowner nearby, belonging to the same clan. Since the father of the bride had no son, the alliance was designed to consolidate Virendra's estate; besides, the bride was beautiful. Therefore the match seemed most attractive to the old man; he proceeded to make arrangements for the wedding. But disregarding his father's choice, Virendra secretly married the daughter of a poor sonless widow from the village, and refused to marry a second time. Furious, the old man disowned his son, evicting him from the family home. Banished by his father, the young man departed for Delhi with the aspiration of becoming a professional soldier. Since his wife was pregnant at the time, she could not accompany him. She stayed behind at her mother's home.

When his son went into exile, the aged landowner was assailed by grief; overcome by remorse, he devoted himself—unsuccessfully—to discover his son's whereabouts. Unable to ensure his son's return, he lovingly brought his daughter-in-law home instead from her poor abode. In due course, Virendrasingh's wife gave birth to a daughter. But the mother died soon afterwards.

Arriving in Delhi, Virendrasingh was employed as a soldier by the Rajput troops who served the Mughal emperor; very soon, his prowess paved the way to a high rank. After he had amassed considerable wealth as well as fame over the next few years, Virendrasingh received news of his father's demise. Thereupon he considered further sojourn in foreign lands or serving as a vassal unnecessary, and returned home. Several of his associates accompanied him from Delhi, among them a maid and a sage. It will be necessary to reveal more about them. The maid's name was Bimala, and the sage's, Swami Abhiram.

Bimala was engaged in housework, in particular bringing up and nurturing Virendra's daughter. There was no other obvious reason for her to live in the fort; hence she has been referred to as a maid. However, she displayed no signs of being one. The occupants of the fort revered her almost as much as a queen would have been revered; all of them were obedient to her. Her appearance suggested that she had been exceptionally beautiful in her younger days. Like the moon that sets only after the sun dawns, the glow of that loveliness was visible even at this age. Swami Abhiram had a disciple named Gajapati Vidya Diggaj—or Gajapati the master scholar. He may or may not have been adept at the art of rhetoric, but his appetite for coarse humour was rather strong. Whenever he set eyes on Bimala he would say, 'She is like butter in a jar; the more the flames of ardor cool, the richer her body becomes.' It is necessary to mention here that since the day Gajapati the scholar had made this droll observation, Bimala had referred to him as the 'Wondrous Witmaster.'

Besides the way she conducted herself, the polished behavior and skilful conversation for which Bimala was regarded could not possibly have been attained by a mere maid. Many people said that she had been a long-standing member of the Mughal emperor's household. Only Bimala knew whether this was the truth or a lie, but she never referred to it.

Was Bimala married or a widow? No one knows. She wore ornaments, didn't observe any widow's rituals, and led her life as married women do.

We have already seen in the temple how deeply Bimala loved Tilottama, the chieftain's daughter. Tilottama adored her just as much. Swami Abhiram, Virendrasingh's other companion from Delhi, did not live at the fort permanently, setting off every now and then to travel around the country.

He took turns between Fort Mandaran and his travels, spending a month or two at each. Everyone was convinced that Swami Abhiram was Virendrasingh's spiritual guru; certainly the respect and honour that Virendrasingh accorded him suggested as much. Why, he did not conduct even his daily tasks without seeking Swami Abhiram's counsel, which inevitably proved prescient. Swami Abhiram was, in fact, far-sighted and possessed razor-sharp intelligence; moreover, he had mastered the art of restraining his passions whether in pursuing his mission or in his everyday behaviour. When required, he could control suppress anger or hatred or displeasure and discuss matters dispassionately. It was not surprising, therefore, that his advice yielded better results than the impetuous and conceited Virendrasingh's strategies.

Besides Bimala and Swami Abhiram, a maid named Aasmani had also accompanied Virendrasingh back home.

Chapter Six

Swami Abhiram's Counsel

TILOTTAMA AND BIMALA returned to the fort safely from the temple. Three or four days later Swami Abhiram arrived at Virendrasingh's court. Virendrasingh rose from his throne and bowed, Swami Abhiram took his seat on the spun-grass mat offered to him by the chieftain, who resumed his position on the throne after seeking permission. 'Virendra!' said Swami Abhiram, 'I wish to discuss an important matter with you today.'

'I await your command,' answered Virendra.

'An intense battle between the Mughals and the Pathans at hand,' announced Swami Abhiram.

'Yes, a critical turn in events appears imminent,' Virendra replied.

Abhiram asked, 'Quite possibly. What do you propose to do now?'

'If the enemy appears, we shall beat him back with sheer force,' Virendra declared haughtily.

'I expected nothing less from a brave warrior like you,' responded the sage, speaking as gently as Virendra had spoken aggressively. 'But the thing is, valuer alone does not ensure victory; that comes from strategic alliances. You yourself are second to none as a warrior, but your troops do not number more than a thousand—is there a general who can repel with a thousand soldiers a force one hundred times as large? Both the Mughals and the Pathans have armies a hundredfold larger than yours; you will not succeed in escaping the one without the help of the other. Do not be enraged, consider the situation calmly. How will it benefit you to oppose both the warring parties? Since our enemies vex us, would it not be better to have one enemy rather than two? Therefore, I think, you should side with one of them.'

After a long silence, Virendra said, 'Which of them should I side with?'

'Choose the side that will not lead you to be unrighteous; treason is a great sin, support the king,' answered Swami Abhiram.

Having considered this a few moments, Virendra enquired, 'But who is the king, really? The war between the Mughals and the Pathans is over the kingdom, after all.'

'He who collects the taxes is the king,' answered Swami Abhiram.

'You mean Akbar Shah?'

'But of course.'

Virendrasingh looked enraged; his eyes slowly became bloodshot. Observing the signs, Swami Abhiram said, 'Control your rage, Virendra! I have asked you to pay allegiance to the Emperor of Delhi, not to Mansingh.'

Virendrasingh pointed his left hand at his right arm with a flourish. 'With the blessings gathered at your feet, this hand shall be drenched in Mansingh's blood.'

'Calm yourself,' said Swami Abhiram. 'Do not allow blind rage to come between you and your mission; by all means punish Mansingh for his past crimes, but what use will it be to wage war against Akbar Shah?'

'If I side with Akbar Shah, under which general's command shall I have to fight?' an enraged Virendra continued. 'Which warrior shall I have to help? Whom shall I have to pay allegiance to? None other than Mansingh. My lord! As long as there's life in this body, Virendrasingh shall never to do it.'

23

Swami Abhiram lapsed into an unhappy silence. After some time he asked, 'Then you would prefer to side with the Pathans?'

'Is it necessary to choose one over the other?'

Abhiram responded, 'Yes, it is.'

Virendra replied, 'Then it is preferable to side with the Pathans.'

Sighing, Swami Abhiram fell silent again; tears appeared in his eyes. Surprised beyond belief, Virendrasingh exclaimed, 'Forgive me, my lord. Tell me how I have unknowingly transgressed.'

Wiping his eyes with his cloak, Swami Abhiram said, 'Listen closely. For several days I have been engaged in astrological calculations. As you know, your daughter is even more the object of my affection than you are; naturally, most of my forecasts concern her.' Virendrasingh turned pale; impatiently, he asked the sage, 'What do your predictions forecast?' 'They forecast great misfortune for Tilottama,' answered the sage, 'caused by a Mughal general.' Virendrasingh's face darkened. 'Only if the Mughals are ranged against you can they bring misfortune upon Tilottama,' Swami Abhiram continued, 'but not if they are allied with you, which is why I tried to induce you to support them. I did not wish to make you suffer by stating this; but human effort is bound to fail, what is written by fate must be, or else why would you prove so adamant?'

Virendrasingh was silent. Swami Abhiram told him, 'Katlu Khan's messenger is at the gate, Virendra. I came to you as soon as I saw him, after instructing the guards not to let him into your presence. Now that I have said what I had to, you may summon the messenger and offer a suitable response.' With a deep sigh, Virendrasingh raised his eyes. 'My lord! Till such time as I had set eyes on Tilottama, I had not even considered her my daughter. Now I have no one except her to call my own; I shall obey your command, I hereby repudiate my past. I will swear allegiance to Mansingh, let the guards bring the messenger to me.'

As instructed, the guards escorted him in. The messenger handed over Katlu Khan's letter. The essence of the missive was that Virendrasingh should dispatch one thousand soldiers on horseback and five thousand gold coins to the Pathan camp, failing which Katlu Khan would send twenty thousand soldiers to besiege Fort Mandaran.

Having read the letter, Virendrasingh said, 'Herald! Inform your master that he may send his troops.' Bowing, the messenger left.

Hidden from view, Bimala had eavesdropped on the entire exchange.

Chapter Seven

Carelessness

TILOTTAMA SAT AT a window, watching the river Amodar murmur as it washed over the fortress, eddies forming in the blue water. Dusk had fallen; the reflection of violet clouds, tinged with the gold of the sun's fading light in the western sky, trembled amidst the rapid currents. The colossal fort by the river, with its rows of tall trees, looked like a picture against the pristine blue of the sky. Inside the fort, peacocks, cranes, and songbirds trilled cheerfully; birds flew silently towards their nests at the advent of night. The summer breeze cooled by the river, rustled through the mangroves and Tilottama's hair or through the beautiful garment draped over her shoulders.

Tilottama was a beauty. O reader! Have you ever beheld in your youth, with the light of love in your eyes, a serene, soft-hearted young girl flowering into womanhood? Have you ever seen a young woman whom you have not been able to forget all your life even though you glanced at her but once— an enchanting figure who treads your memory over and over again like a dream, through adolescence youth and maturity, through work and through rest, and yet does not provoke a tainting desire? Only if you have will Tilottama's true image come to life in your mind's eye. Hers was neither the plenitude of beauty that enkindles your heart, nor the seductive charm that sinks poisonous fangs into it. Instead, hers was the image that delights with its tenderness and grace. The image that sways in the memory like the vines of spring do in the evening breeze.

Tilottama was sixteen, which meant her body had not yet acquired the fullness of the woman who has matured already. Both her body and her face still held some traces of childhood. Her shapely, curved, generous—but not too generous—forehead radiated the tranquillity of the river lit by moonlight. Her short, dark ringlets fell on her eyebrows, her cheeks, her neck, her shoulders, her breasts. There was a disciplined profusion of rich, dark hair on her back. Beneath her forehead her eyebrows were well arched, dark, as though painted by an artist, and yet a little too slender—being just a hair's-breadth thicker would have made them flawless. Do you love restless eyes, reader? Then Tilottama will not be able to conquer your heart. Tilottama's eyes were exceedingly placid; they threw no glances like bolts of lightning. Her eyes were wide, lovely, shining with a serene glow. And their colour was the tender shade of blue that permeates the sky shortly before sunrise, when the moon is about to set. When Tilottama bestowed a glance from those wide, clear eyes, it held not the slightest trace of guile. Tilottama was not versed in the art of throwing arch looks. Her gaze held nothing but purity and simplicity—simplicity in her eyes and simplicity in her heart. If anyone looked at her, however, her soft lashes dropped at once; Tilottama never looked anywhere but at the ground when she was noticed. Her lips were pink, brimming moistly; small, a little rounded, a little swollen, smiling. Were you to see a smile on those lips but once, whether you be a yogi or a sage, old or young, you would not be able to forget it, even though the smile was nothing but simple and childlike.

Although shapely, Tilottama's body was not yet ripe; whether it was because of her youth or because of her natural build, her beautiful frame displayed the qualities only of slenderness. And yet there was nothing angular in any aspect of her slim body. Jewels adorned her lovely wrists, diamond-studded bracelets sat on her lovely arms, rings were set around

27

her lovely fingers, an ornamental girdle covered her lovely thighs, golden ornaments covered her lovely shoulders, jewel-encrusted necklaces encircled her lovely throat. Every part of her was beautiful.

What was Tilottama doing by herself at the window? Was she gazing upon the beauty of the evening? Then why were her eyes downcast? Was she taking the fragrant breeze wafting in from the river bank? Then why would there be beads of perspiration on her brow? The breeze was fanning but one side of her face—why? Was she watching the cows graze? But no, the cows had all wended their way homewards. Was she listening to the cuckoo? Why so sad, then? Tilottama saw nothing, heard nothing, she was lost in thought.

The maid lit the lamps. Her musing completed, Tilottama sat down by a lamp with a book. She knew how to read, having learnt Sanskrit from Swami Abhiram. She was reading *Kadambari**. After a few pages, she abandoned *Kadambari*, in annoyance fetching another book in its stead, *Basavadatta** by Subandhu. She alternated between reading and thinking. She did not find Basavadatta to her taste either. Forsaking it, she took up *Geetgovindam***, which she enjoyed for a few minutes before flinging it away with a shy smile. After that she sat on her bed, restless. A quill and inkpot lay close at hand; seizing them, she started writing on the wooden surface of the bed absent-mindedly: she wrote the letters for K, S, and M, along with drawings of houses, doors, trees, people, and so on. Eventually the entire side of the bed was filled with her calligraphy. When there was no more space, she came to her senses. Laughing lightly at her handiwork, she proceeded to

---

*Famous Sanskrit love stories.
**The great book of poetry that celebrates the love of Krishna and Radha. It was composed by the twelfth century Oriya poet, Jayadev.

read what she had written, giggling. What had she written and drawn? Basavadatta, Mahashweta, the letters for K, E, E, and P, a tree, an idol of Shiva, *Geetgovindam*, Bimala, leaves, vines, some gibberish, the fort...heavens, what was this!... Prince Jagatsingh.

Tilottama blushed in shame. Silly! Why should she be embarrassed when there was no one else in the room?

Prince Jagatsingh. Tilottama read the words once, twice, several times. She stole glances at the door as she read, as though she were a thief.

She did not linger very long, however, in case someone saw her. Quickly fetching water, she washed the ink off. Still not satisfied she wiped it again carefully with her garment. She tried to read her scribbles once more, saw that there was no trace of the ink left, yet still felt the words could be read. Again she washed it with water, wiped it once more with her garment, and yet she still could not help feeling the words were clearly visible—Prince Jagatsingh.

Chapter Eight

Bimala's Proposal

BIMALA STOOD INSIDE Swami Abhiram's hut. He was seated on the floor in a yogic position. She described Jagatsingh's encounter with her and Tilottama in detail; completing her accounts, she said, 'It is the fourteenth day today; the fortnight ends tomorrow.' 'What have you decided?' asked Swami Abhiram.

'I am here for your wise counsel,' answered Bimala.

'Excellent,' responded the sage. 'My advice is not to think about this any more.'

Bimala remained silent, looking disheartened. 'Why do you look dejected?' asked Swami Abhiram.

'What will happen to Tilottama?' said Bimala.

'What! Is Tilottama infatuated with the young man?' exclaimed the sage in surprise.

'If only you knew,' Bimala said after a few moments of silence. 'I have kept Tilottama under close observation these past two weeks, and it appears to me that she is deeply in love.'

'You women,' commented the sage with a wry smile, 'interpret the smallest sign of infatuation as passionate love. Do not worry for Tilottama's happiness, Bimala; she is young—naturally she has become enamoured of the young man at first sight; as long as the subject is not brought up, she will soon forget Jagatsingh.'

'No, my lord, there is no such sign. Tilottama has changed much in a mere fortnight. She no longer laughs and jokes with me or other girls of her age in the fort as she was wont to do. She has virtually stopped speaking. Her books are rotting beneath her bed, her flowers are dying because they have not been watered. Tilottama does not look after her birds any more or eat or sleep at night. She no longer dresses up. Tilottama was never one to be lost in her thoughts, but now she is sunk in them day and night. Tilottana's visage bears the shadow sorrow.'

Swami Abhiram was silenced. After some time he said, 'I had always thought there was no such thing as love at first sight. However, God alone understands women, especially young women. But what will you do? Virendra will never agree to this match.'

'I fear as much, which is why I have not brought the subject up yet,' answered Bimala. 'Nor did I reveal our identities to Jagatsingh in the temple. But if Lord Singh'—there was a change in Bimala's expression—'if Lord Singh were to form an alliance with Mansingh, what harm would it do to accept Jagatsingh as his son-in-law?'

A: But why will Mansingh agree either?

B: Let him not, the prince is free to choose.

A: Why will Jagatsingh marry Virendrasingh's daughter, for that matter?

B: There is nothing in the ancestry on either side that forbids it, Jaidharsingh's forefathers also trace their lineage back to the clan of Krishna.'

A: You expect a woman whose lineage goes back to Krishna to marry a Muslim's brother-in-law's son?'

'Why not?' retorted Bimala, looking intently at the ascetic. 'Is any branch of Krishna's family to be abhorred?'

No sooner had she spoken than the sage's eyes blazed in anger. Sternly, he said, 'Sinner! So you have not forgotten your own sorry fate? Leave this room this instant!'

Chapter Nine

The Glory of the Clan

IN THE FORTNIGHT he had left his father's protection, Jagatsingh's exploits were such as to strike terror in the hearts of the Pathan army, although he had not as yet succeeded in his vow to drive Katlu Khan's fifty-thousand-strong army back to the opposite bank of the Subarnarekha with his five thousand. When Mansingh heard of his son's military prowess he said, 'Perhaps the original glory of the Rajput clan will be restored by my prince.'

Jagatsingh knew perfectly well that it was impossible to repel fifty thousand soldiers in full frontal battle with five thousand—on the contrary, defeat or death was inevitable. Thus instead of attempting such a confrontation, he adopted strategies to prevent it. He kept his handful of troops hidden, selecting concealed spots for his camps—either inside dense forests or the hills of the region, with its troughs and crests like ocean waves—so that they were invisible even close at hand. He remained out of sight in this manner, descending with his troops like an avalanche on small companies of Pathan soldiers whenever he received news of their presence, decimating them completely. He engaged spies to roam the countryside disguised as fruit, vegetable, or fish vendors, or as beggars, ascetics, sages, and physicians, to bring him intelligence about the movement of Pathan troops. As soon as he had received his information, Jagatsingh would station his troops with great secrecy and swiftness at a locale where he could remain unseen and launch a tactical attack. If the company of Pathan soldiers proved larger than estimated, he made no attempt to besiege them, for he knew that a single defeat would mean the end of his entire campaign. In those instances he only stalked them cautiously to seize the enemy's ammunition and horses after they had left. And if the quarry was not very large in numbers, he would lie in wait till the Pathans had reached the area where he wanted to attack them. Then, seizing the right moment, his soldiers would pursue them like roaring, hungry tigers, tearing them to pieces. Unaware of their foes, the Pathans were never prepared for battle. Suddenly assailed by a wave of enemy soldiers, they would almost always lose their lives without even putting up a fight.

Countless Pathan soldiers were slain in this manner. Greatly alarmed, the Pathans attempted to engage Jagatsingh's troops in open battle and destroy them. But they could not track down the whereabouts of Jagatsingh's army; like messengers of death, they only made a single appearance at the final hour of their victims, disappearing after completing the ritual of slaughter. The wily Jagatsingh never kept all his five thousand soldiers together. He dispatched them in small groups—a thousand here, five hundred there, two hundred or two thousand elsewhere—wherever the enemy had been observed; and moved them away as soon as the mission was accomplished. The Pathans simply could not pin the Rajputs down to a particular location. Katlu Khan kept receiving news of casualties every single day. As a result, it became impossible for Pathan soldiers to venture out of the fort in small numbers, even if the task at hand was slight. Plunder and pillage stopped altogether; all the soldiers took refuge within the fortresses, even gathering food became difficult. When informed of the way in which his son was bringing order to the lands under enemy attack, Mansingh wrote him a letter:

'Pride of the family! I am convinced you shall deliver the kingdom from the clutches of the Pathans; accordingly I am dispatching another ten thousand soldiers to support your war.'

The prince replied:

'As Your Majesty wishes. Reinforcements will be welcome; but even without them, your servant will fulfil the vow that he made at your feet with the same five thousand soldiers, as befits a member of the Kshatriya clan.'

Intoxicated by the heady brew of valour, the prince won a succession of battles. O Lord of the Mountains! Amidst the din of war, has the brave warrior not recalled even once the beautiful young woman in your temple whose innocent gaze had conquered him? If he has not, he too is made of stone like you.

Chapter Ten

After the Proposal, Action

It was the morning after Swami Abhiram had evicted Bimala from his room in anger. She was in her chambers dressing up. A thirty-five-year-old woman dressing up? But why not? Can age kill youth? Youth is killed by the lack of beauty, it is killed in the mind. The woman who is not beautiful is old at twenty; the woman who is, can be young at any age. She whose heart is dry is always middle-aged, she whose isn't, is perennially youthful. Even today Bimala was voluptuously beautiful, exceptionally passionate. Age matures passion, as any reader who is a little advanced in years will surely acknowledge.

Who could claim after a glimpse of Bimala's paan-reddened lips that she was not young? Who could say after catching a fleeting glance from her generous kohl-smudged eyes that she was a day over twenty-four? And what eyes! Elongated, animated, entrancing. There are some women whose eyes instantly make you think that they are haughty and arrogant, that they are committed pleasure-seekers. Such were Bimala's eyes. I can assure the reader with certainty that Bimala was a young woman, you could even say time stood still for her. Who would contend after sensing the gentleness of her jasmine-white skin that a sixteen-year-old's skin was gentler? Who would suggest after a glimpse of the tiny, ever so tiny, curl that had escaped from behind her ear to fall on her cheek that it was not the cheek of a young woman on which the curl lay? Open the eye of your mind, O reader! Cast it on Bimala as she sits before her mirror, attending to her hair. See how she has gathered her long locks in her left hand to comb them. See how she is smiling at her own vivacity. Listen to the sweet melodies she occasionally hums in a honeyed voice. Observe all of this closely, and then tell me whether you would still prefer a younger woman.

After combing her hair, Bimala did not leave it loose; instead she made a long braid out of it. She wiped her face on a perfumed handkerchief, reddened her lips again with rosewater- and camphor-flavoured paan, put on her pearl-studded bodice, covered herself with her gold ornaments, and then, on second thoughts, took off some of them. She dressed herself in intricately embroidered garments, slipped on pearl-encrusted sandals, and finally, wove the prince's gift—the valuable necklace—into her immaculately coiffed hair.

Completing her toilette, Bimala proceeded to Tilottama's room. Tilottama was astonished at the sight of her, asking with a smile, 'What is all this, Bimala! Why are you dressed this way?'

'What business is it of yours?' countered Bimala.

T: Tell me, please, where are you going?

B: Who told you I am going anywhere?

Tilottama was embarrassed. Seeing her reaction, Bimala said with a pale smile, 'I am going far away.'

Tilottama's face bloomed with joy like a happily unfolding lotus. 'Where?' she asked softly.

'Guess,' said Bimala, smiling slyly.

Tilottama looked at her uncomprehendingly.

Taking her hand, Bimala drew her to the window, saying, 'I will tell you.' Then she whispered in her ear, 'I am going to the temple of Shiva. I shall meet a certain prince there.'

Tilottama felt a thrill running through her. She said nothing.

'I discussed this with Swami Abhiram,' continued Bimala. 'He considers marriage between you and Jagatsingh impossible. Your father will never agree. If the issue is raised in his presence, I will be lucky to escape a flogging.'

'Then why?' Her eyes downcast, gazing at the floor, Tilottama uttered just these two words in a stifled voice. 'Then why?'

B: Why? I had agreed to meet the prince tonight and reveal our identity. But what will he do with the information alone? Let me tell him who we are, then he can do what he has to. If the prince is enamoured of you…'

Covering her face and not allowing Bimala to finish, Tilottama said, 'You embarrass me. Go wherever you like, but do not tell anyone about me, and do not tell me about anyone either.'

Smiling again, Bimala asked, 'Then why have you plunged into this ocean at such a tender age?'

'Go away. I am not listening to anything you say,' said Tilottama.

Bimala said, 'Then I need not go to the temple.'

T: Have I stopped you from going? Go wherever you want to.

'Then I will not go,' said Bimala, laughing.

Lowering her eyes to the floor again, Tilottama said, 'Go.' Bimala started laughing again. After a while, she said, 'I am going now, do not go to sleep till I am back.'

Tilottama smiled too, its meaning clear: 'Do you suppose I can sleep?' Bimala understood. Before leaving, she put one hand on Tilottama's shoulder and held up her face with the other; gazing upon her pure, love-struck face briefly, she kissed her tenderly. Tilottama spotted a tear in Bimala's eye as she made to leave.

Arriving at the door, Aasmani told Bimala, 'The master has summoned you.'

37

'Change your clothes before you go,' whispered Tilottama to Bimala.

'Do not worry,' responded Bimala.

She went to Virendrasingh's bedroom. He was lying back in his bed, a maid massaging his feet and another fanning him. Approaching the bed, she said, 'What is your command?'

Lifting his head, Virendrasingh was wonderstruck. 'Are you going somewhere, Bimala?' he asked.

'Yes,' Bimala responded. 'Any instructions for me?'

V: How is Tilottama? She was ill, has she recovered?

B: She has.

V: Fan me for a few minutes while Aasmani fetches Tilottama.

The maid with the fan put it down and left.

Bimala signalled Aasmani to wait outside the room. 'Go and make some paan for me, Lachhmani,' Virendrasingh instructed the other maid, who was massaging his foot. She left.

V: Why are you dressed in this way today, Bimala?

B: There is a reason.

V: I want to know.

'Then you shall,' said Bimala, casting a glance at Virendra with the love god smouldering in her eyes. 'I am going on a tryst.'

V: Not with death, I hope.

B: Can I not have a tryst with a man?

V: The man has not been born yet.

B: Besides one.

She left swiftly.

38

Chapter Eleven

Aasmani the Messenger

MEANWHILE, AASMANI WAS waiting for Bimala as instructed. 'I have something to tell you in private, Aasmani,' Bimala told her.

'I was convinced from the way you are dressed that something is afoot,' Aasmani replied.

'I will be travelling some distance on a special mission,' Bimala said. 'I cannot go by myself at this hour of the night, nor can I trust anyone but you to come with me. So you must accompany me.'

'Where are you going?' enquired Aasmani.

'You were not prone to asking so many questions before,' observed Bimala.

'Will you wait a little then,' said a subdued Aasmani. 'I will complete my chores.'

'One more thing,' added Bimala. 'Suppose you were to meet someone from the past today, would they be able to recognize you?'

'What do you mean?' exclaimed Aasmani in surprise.

'Suppose you were to meet Prince Jagatsingh,' said Bimala.

'Will such a day ever dawn,' exclaimed Aasmani in pleasure.

'Well, it might,' replied Bimala.

'Of course the prince will recognize me,' Aasmani told her.

'Then you must not come,' said Bimala. 'But whom can I ask—and yet I cannot go alone either.'

'I long to meet the prince,' confessed Aasmani.

'Keep your longing to yourself,' retorted Bimala. 'What do I do now?'

While Bimala pondered, Aasmani suddenly covered her mouth with her hand and began to giggle. 'Damn you,' exploded Bimala. 'What on earth are you laughing yourself to death for?'

'I was wondering whether to send our golden boy Diggaj with you,' said Aasmani chuckling.

'That is an excellent idea.' Bimala laughed in elation. 'Yes, I shall take our clown prince.'

'But it was a joke!' interjected Aasmani.

'It is not a joke, I trust the foolish Brahmin completely. Just as the blind man cannot tell day apart from night, he too will understand nothing. So there is no reason to fear him. But he will not be willing to come along.'

'Leave it to me.' Aasmani chuckled. 'I will bring him, will you wait for us at the gate?'

Still chuckling, she disappeared in the direction of a small hut within the fort.

The reader has already been acquainted with Swami Abhiram's disciple Gajapati Vidya Diggaj. The reader is aware, too, of why Bimala had dubbed him the Witmaster. The hut was occupied by this august person. The scholar was about six and a half feet tall, but no more than nine inches wide. His legs measured over four feet from the waist downwards, but were only as thick as a slim tree stump. His complexion was that of ink; it seemed as though the fire god had mistaken his legs for timber and began to consume them, but discarded them halfway after finding them lacking in flavour. Because of his excessive height, he stooped a little. The most prominent feature on his face was his nose, where the body had compensated for its lack of flesh elsewhere. His head was unevenly shaven, the bristles that remained were close-cropped, needle-sharp. The Brahmin's ritual tail of hair on his shaved pate pointed upwards proudly.

Gajapati had not received his title of Vidya Diggaj, the master-scholar, by his own choice. He was sharply intelligent. He had begun his study of classical grammar when still a boy, completing the preliminaries in seven tortuous months. Aided by the kindness of his teacher and the din raised by other students, he mastered the first course in fifteen years. Before allowing him to embark on the next course, the teacher chose to survey the terrain that lay before his student. 'Can you tell me the declensions of Rama?' he asked. After much thought, the boy answered, 'Ramakanta.' 'You are extremely well versed in grammar, my boy,' declared the teacher, 'you need not study any more. You may go home now. I have no more knowledge to offer you.'

Gajapati said conceitedly, 'I have but one request—what of my title?'

'The knowledge you have acquired demands a special title, my boy,' the teacher told him. 'I confer the title of Vidya Diggaj—scholar supreme—upon you.'

Pleased, Diggaj bade a respectful farewell to his teacher before wending his way homeward.

'Now that I have mastered grammar,' mused Diggaj at home, 'it is imperative to read some classical scriptures. I have been told Swami Abhiram is a great scholar, no one but he can be a suitable teacher for me, and I should educate myself with his guidance.' Thus he ensconced himself within the fort. Swami Abhiram taught many students without allowing himself to be annoyed by any of them. Whether Diggaj learnt anything or not, he went on giving him his lessons.

Gajapati was not only adept at grammar and at reciting the scriptures from memory, he was also a rhetorician, a bit of a wit, flattery was his natural skill. He was particularly full of wit in his exchanges with Aasmani. Behind this lay some deeper significance. Gajapati had convinced himself that he had been born like Krishna for sport and dalliance, that his abode was but his playground, the equivalent of Krishna's Vrindavan, and that Aasmani's relationship with him was the same amorous one as Radha's with Krishna. Aasmani had a sense of humour too, deriving from this present-day incarnate of Madanmohan the same pleasure that a pet monkey offered. Bimala too made the monkey dance sometimes. 'I have found my companions in love,' Diggaj would muse. 'And why not? Their heads have been turned by my compliments; how fortunate that Bimala has no idea that they are borrowed.'

Chapter Twelve

Aasmani's Tryst

THE ESTEEMED READER is undoubtedly curious to know what manner of beauty Aasmani, conqueror of Gajapati Diggaj, was. I shall satiate your curiosity. However, it would be impudent for an insignificant individual like myself to deviate from the convention normally followed by authors when describing the beauty of women. Therefore, I must first invoke the goddess.

O goddess of speech. O lotus-seated one. O autumnal moon. O patroness of devotees at your feet outshining the whitest of lotus petals. The shade of those lotus-feet; I shall describe Aasmani's beauty. O you who shrinks the pride of the clan of lovely, lotus-faced women. O creator of the succulent potato-metaphor! Grant me but an insignificant corner in your proximity, so that I may describe beauty. I shall prepare a repast of potato-compound, eggplant, blend and plantain simile to serve the bedgeree up to thee. O fount of wisdom desired by the learned classes. O you who occasionally look kindly upon the ignorant. O creator of the frenzy of feverishly itching fingers. O fuel-supplier to sensational writers' lamps of learning. Kindle the lamp of my intelligence once, I pray to you. O goddess! You have two forms. Pray do not vex me by straddling my shoulders in the form in which you blessed Kalidasa, whose influence gave birth to *Raghuvamsham*, to *Kumarsambhavam*, to *Meghdootam*, to *Shakuntalam*, the spirit whose devoted pursuit led Valmiki to compose the *Ramayana*; Bhababhuti, the *Uttararamacharita*; Bharavi, the *Kiratarjuniya*.

Descend upon my shoulders instead in the form which inspired the Sriharsha to compose the *Naishadharcharitram*, which inspired Bharatchandra to describe the exquisite beauty of Vidya, captivating all of Bengal, whose benediction gave birth to the divine fervour of Dasarathi Roy, the spirit which still lights up the world of popular literature, so that I may describe Aasmani's beauty.

Aasmani's braided hair was like a coiled snake. If I must be defeated by a braid, the snake muttered to itself in ignominy, of what use is this body of mine? Let me retreat into my hole. The Lord sensed trouble—if the snake was going to stay in its hole, who would bite humans? He pulled the snake out by its tail, whereupon the creature, humiliated at having to reveal its face to the world again, battered its head against the ground repeatedly. The snake's head has remained flat ever since. Because Aasmani was more beautiful, the moon, unable to rise, complained to the Lord bitterly. Fear not, said the Lord, you may rise, women shall veil their faces from now on —and that was when the veil was created. Her eyes were like wagtails—lest they spread their wings and escape, the Creator has incarcerated them in a prison of lashes. Her nose was shapelier than the mythical Garuda's, who promptly retired to treetops to hide its disgrace—birds have lived on trees since then. The pomegranate, symbol of the bosom found itself with no choice but to escape to the Patna region; the elephant migrated to Burma with its bullous head; that left the Dhaulagiri, which compared the height of its own peak to hers and found itself falling short by a mile, whereupon it became so agitated that it needed a mound of snow on its head to quieten—and has remained snow-capped ever since.

By an unfortunate turn of destiny, Aasmani was a widow. Arriving at Diggaj's hut, she found the door barred and a lamp burning within. 'Are you in, O Master?' she called.

There was no answer.

'Are you there, O divine disciple?'

Still no answer.

'What on earth is the rogue doing? Are you within, O jester supreme?'

Nothing.

Peeping through a hole in the door, Aasmani saw the good Brahmin sitting down to his meal. That was why he was silent, for once he has spoken during a meal, a Brahmin may eat no more. 'Him and faithful! Let me find out if he really will not eat any more once he has spoken,' Aasmani thought to herself.

'Listen to me, O poet!'

No answer—'O poet'.

Answer: Hmm.

The good Brahmin was grunting with food in his mouth —that was not tantamount to speaking. 'O jewel on earth,' Aasmani called again, determined to break his silence.

Answer: Hmm.

A: Why don't you talk to me, you can eat later.

Answer: Hm…mm…mm!

A: You call yourself a Brahmin but you're up to mischief. I'm going to tell the swami—who is that in the room with you?

Terrified, the good Brahmin surveyed his room quickly. Seeing it was empty, he resumed eating.

'That hussy is an untouchable,' declared Aasmani. 'I know her well!'

'Untouchable? Has she touched anything?' the good Brahmin gasped.

'So you are eating again? After you spoke?' Aasmani asked triumphantly.

D: When did I speak?

'There! You just did!' Aasmani broke into peals of laughter.

D: Indeed. Indeed. I cannot eat any more.

A: That is right. Now open the door for me.

Peering through the hole, Aasmani saw the good Brahmin had indeed abandoned his meal. 'Why do you not finish your meal first?' she suggested.

D: No, I cannot eat any more.

A: Please do, I beg of you.

D: Lord, lord, how can I eat after I have spoken?

A: Really? Then I am off. There was so much I had to tell you, but it is impossible now. I am off.

D: No, Aasmani, do not be angry. I will eat.

The good Brahmin resumed his meal. After he had swallowed two or three mouthfuls, Aasmani said, 'Enough, open the door now.'

D: Let me finish.

A: You have a bottomless pit for a stomach. Get up now, or I will tell everyone you went on eating after you spoke.

D: Oh, such a bother. Alright, I am coming.

Abandoning his meal gloomily, the good Brahmin rinsed his hands and opened the door.

Chapter Thirteen

Aasmani's Romance

AASMANI ENTERED AS soon as he opened the door. It dawned on Diggaj that his beloved deserved a worthy welcome. Therefore, he intoned in Sanskrit, his arm upraised, 'I bow in reverence to you, O goddess.'

'And where did you discover such juicy poetry?' enquired Aasmani.

D: I composed it today just for you.

A: Not for nothing have I dubbed you the king of amours.

D: Sit down, O beautiful lady. Allow me to wash my hands.

'By the gods,' murmured Aasmani to herself. 'Rinse your hands if you like, I shall still make you finish the leftovers.'

For his benefit, she said, 'But why? Are you not eating any more?'

'What do you mean, I have just completed my meal, how can I eat again?' said Gajapati.

A: But there is all that rice left on your plate. Are you planning to starve?

'You hurried me so,' answered Diggaj, somewhat aggrieved. He gazed hungrily at his plate of rice.

'Then you must eat again,' declared Aasmani.

D: By the lord, I have rinsed my mouth, left my seat, how can I eat again?

'Of course you shall eat. And that too, off my plate.' Announcing this, Aasmani took a mouthful of rice.

The good Brahmin stared in surprise.

'Eat,' Aasmani instructed him, pointing to the plate she had just used.

The good Brahmin was speechless.

A: Go on, eat, I will not tell anyone you ate off my plate. As long as no one gets to know, you have not broken any rules.

D: How is that possible?

But hunger was raging in Diggaj's belly. His secret wish at the moment was that, be Aasmani ever so beautiful, the earth should open up and swallow her, so that he could surreptitiously eat the rest of the rice to appease his burning hunger.

Sensing what was going through his mind, Aasmani said, 'Never mind, whether you eat or not, go take your seat before the plate.'

D: Why? What purpose will that serve?

A: It is my dearest wish. Can you not fulfil even a single wish of mine?

'Very well, it will do no harm to merely sit by the plate, I can do that easily enough,' declared Diggaj. 'I shall honour your wish.' Complying with Aasmani's request, he sat down again before his plate of food. His stomach was growling, the rice was within his reach, but still he was unable to eat— Diggaj felt tears pricking his eyelids.

'What must a Brahmin do if he eats off a Shudra's plate?' asked Aasmani.

'He must bathe at once,' answered the scholar.

Aasmani said, 'Tonight I shall find out how deeply you love me. Will you bathe at this hour of the night if I ask you to?'

His small eyes half-closed with passion, Diggaj wrinkled his long nose and smiled sweetly from ear to ear. 'But of course. Immediately, if you so desire.'

'I have a craving to share your food,' murmured Aasmani. 'Feed me yourself.'

'And why not, indeed, since all it will need is a bath to cleanse me,' responded Diggaj. He proceeded to divide up the rice—which Aasmani had already tasted—into small portions.

'Let me tell you a tale, meanwhile,' said Aasmani. 'You must not feed me till I have finished.'

D: Very well.

Aasmani began a story of a king and his two wives. Diggaj listened in rapt attention, while his hands worked on the rice of their own volition.

As he listened, his attention remained riveted somewhere between her smile, her coy glances, and her nose stud. His hands stopped moving, but they remained on the plate, while his hunger continued to torment him. When Aasmani's tale neared the climax, so absorbed was Diggaj in the outcome that his hands betrayed him. They raised a portion of rice from the plate to his mouth, which promptly opened wide to accept it. The teeth proceeded to chew on it without demur. The tongue pushed it down his gullet, poor Diggaj not protesting in the least. Aasmani broke into peals of laughter. 'And so you rogue, did you not claim that you would never eat my leftovers?' she taunted him.

Diggaj came to his senses. After swallowing another mouthful, he clutched Aasmani's feet, his hands still sticky. 'Save me, Aasmani, pray do not tell anyone,' he moaned as he ate.

Chapter Fourteen

The Kidnapping of Vidya Diggaj

SUDDENLY BIMALA ARRIVED and knocked on the door. She had been observing everything secretly through a side door. Diggaj's face paled at the sound. 'Oh my god, Bimala is here,' exclaimed Aasmani. 'Quick, hide.'

'Where?' wailed Diggaj.

'Go sit in that corner with the black pot over your head,' advised Aasmani, 'you will not be visible in the darkness.' Wonderstruck at Aasmani's incisive thinking, he attempted to comply. Unfortunately he chose a pot of daal to upturn on his head—it was half-full; as he was about to use it for cover, streams of lentils gushed out, running in torrents down his tail of hair—like a river surging down the mountain towards the plains, orange currents of daal cascaded in waves down his shoulders, chest, back, and arms. His lofty nose stood proudly like a mountain peak dotted with waterfalls of orange daal. Bimala entered the room and gazed upon the sight that Diggaj presented. He sobbed when he saw her. She was moved to pity. 'Do not cry,' she said. 'If you eat the rest of the leftover rice, we will not disclose anything to anyone.'

The Brahmin grew cheerful, resuming his meal joyfully, he wished he could mop up the daal clinging to his body, but was unable to—or perhaps didn't dare to. He consumed the rice he had set out for Aasmani, lamenting over the wasted daal. After his meal Aasmani gave him a bath. Then, when he had settled down quietly, Bimala said, 'There is something important I have to tell you, Witmaster.'

'What?' asked the Witmaster.

B: Do you love us?

D: Of course.

B: Both of us?

D: Both of you.

B: Can you do what I want you to?

D: But of course.

B: Right now?

D: Right now.

B: This instant?

D: This instant.

B: Do you know why both of us are here?

D: No.

B: We want to run away with you.

The good Brahmin gaped at them in astonishment. Bimala suppressed her laughter with supreme effort. 'Why don't you say something?' she asked.

'Er, uh, I, uh, er…' Words would not emerge.

'Then you cannot?' asked Aasmani.

'Er, uh, I, uh, er…let me inform the swami first.'

'What do you mean inform the swami?' said Bimala. 'Are you arranging your mother's funeral and need the swami's help with the arrangements?'

D: No, alright, I will not inform him. When do we have to leave?

B: When? Immediately, can you not see I've brought my jewellery along?

D: Immediately?

B: This instant. If you cannot, say so, we will look for someone else to help us.

Gajapati could contain himself no longer. 'Let us go then,' he said.

51

'Take your shawl,' said Bimala.

Diggaj wrapped his shawl with the holy words woven on them around his shoulders. As Bimala led the way, with the Brahmin bringing up the rear, Vidya Diggaj said, 'My lady!'

B: What?

D: When shall we return?

B: Return! We are leaving forever.

A smile suffusing his face, Diggaj said, 'But the utensils?'

B: I will buy you new ones.

The good Brahmin was disappointed; but he had no choice, what if the ladies concluded he didn't love them. He made one last attempt. 'My books?'

'Quickly,' said Bimala.

The scholar owned just two books—a grammar and a scripture. Picking up the grammar, he said, 'What is the use, I have memorized it.' He took only the scripture. 'May the gods protect us,' he muttered, leaving with Bimala and Aasmani.

'Go on ahead, I will follow,' said Aasmani.

Aasmani went back indoors while Bimala and Gajapati proceeded together. Invisible in the darkness, they made their exit through the gateway to the fort. After they had progressed some distance, Gajapati said, 'Is Aasmani not coming?'

'She could not, it seems. Do we need her?'

Gajapati was silent. 'My utensils,' he sighed after a long pause.

Chapter Fifteen

The Scholar's Courage

WALKING SWIFTLY, BIMALA soon left Mandaran behind. The night was exceedingly dark as she guided herself carefully by starlight. Upon setting foot on the vast open expanse of land leading to the temple, Bimala was somewhat alarmed. Her companion was following her silently, uttering not a word. At such moments the sound of a human voice provides courage, it is even desirable. 'What do you muse upon, jewel among wits?' Bimala asked Gajapati.

'My utensils,' disclosed the master of wit.

Bimala began to giggle silently, covering her face.

'Do you fear ghosts?' Bimala spoke again after a few minutes.

'O lord. Lord O lord O lord,' intoned Diggaj, moving a couple of yards closer to Bimala.

What we get, we want not. 'This road is infested with spirits!' Bimala announced. Diggaj now took hold of the end of Bimala's saree. 'The other evening, on our way back from the Shiva temple, we saw a hideous figure here!'

The quavering at her garment told Bimala that the good Brahmin was trembling uncontrollably. She realized that if she went any further he would be transfixed to the spot. Relenting, she said, 'Can you sing, Diggaj?'

Is there a gallant in the world who is not adept at music? 'But of course,' answered Diggaj.

'Then sing me a song,' commanded Bimala.

'E...Hmm...e...hmm'...Diggaj began...

'What a moment that was, when I saw Shyam on the Kadam tree…'

A cow resting on the grass, contentedly chewing the cud, bolted at top speed on hearing this miraculous music.

The poet continued singing.

'That day spelt my doom, I sullied my family honour.

With his crown and flute and smiles he spoke, shall I tip your pitcher over, milkmaid?'

Diggaj could sing no more, his senses were suddenly captivated. Strains of music ambrosial, transporting, as sweet as the melody of celestial nymphs, drifted into his ears. Bimala was singing, full-throated and clear.

The octaves rose and fell all the way up to the night sky and back over the silent expanse of land. The notes were borne along on the cool summer breeze.

Diggaj listened breathlessly. When Bimala had ended, he said, 'Again.'

B: Again?

D: Sing another song.

B: What should I sing?

D: A Bangla song now.

'Alright,' said Bimala, and resumed singing.

As she sang, Bimala felt a violent tug on her garment. Looking behind her, she discovered Gajapati was almost upon her, clutching her clothes as tight as he could. 'Now what?' asked Bimala in surprise. 'Another ghost?'

The good Brahmin could barely speak. Pointing, he said, 'There.'

In silence, Bimala followed his finger with her eyes. As she noticed an object by the side of the road, she could hear heavy and rapid breathing.

Summoning all the courage at her disposal, she went up to it to discover a well-built, beautifully adorned stallion caught in the throes of death.

Bimala continued on her way, rapt in thought at the sight of the dying beast. She was silent for a long time. When they had walked a mile, Gajapati tugged at her clothes again.

'What is it?' said Bimala.

Gajapati showed her what he was holding. 'It is a soldier's turban,' Bimala said. Deep in thought again, she said to herself, 'Do the turban and the horse belong to the same person? But no, this turban was worn by someone on foot.'

The moon rose after some time. Bimala was even more distracted. After a long interval, Gajapati took courage in his hands. 'Nothing to say, my beauteous lady?'

'Have you noticed any signs on this road?' asked Bimala.

Examining the surface of the road with great care, Gajapati said, 'I can see many hoofprints.'

B: Has the clever gentleman learnt anything from them?'
D: No.

B: A dead horse, a soldier's turban, so many hoofprints, and still you understand nothing? Ah, but who am I talking to!

D: Understand what?

B: Several soldiers have been on this road recently.

'Then let us walk slowly, let them get further away from us,' said Gajapati fearfully.

'Fool,' laughed Bimala. 'How can they be in front of us? Can you not see which way the hoofprints are pointing? These soldiers were travelling towards Fort Mandaran.' She looked apprehensive.

Suddenly the white outline of the Shiva temple appeared before them. Bimala decided there was no need for the good Brahmin to meet the prince—on the contrary, it might lead to trouble. Just as she was wondering how to rid herself of him, Gajapati himself gave her an opportunity.

The good Brahmin was once again clutching at the end of Bimala's scarf. 'What is it now?' she asked.

'How far is it?' the good Brahmin muttered.

55

B: How far is what?

D: The banyan tree.

B: What banyan tree?

D: Where you had seen it the other night?

B: Where I had seen what the other night?

D: You are not supposed to utter its name after sunset.

Bimala saw her chance.

'Oooh,' she shrieked.

'What is it?' asked the good Brahmin, his fear doubling.

'There it is, that banyan tree.' Bimala indicated the tree near the temple.

The scholar froze, rooted to the spot, and then began to tremble like a leaf.

'Come along,' said Bimala.

'I cannot move another step,' the good Brahmin said, shaking with fear.

'I am afraid, too,' declared Bimala.

At this the good Brahmin readied to run back the way he had come.

Glancing at the tree, Bimala spotted something white beneath it. She was aware that the temple bull often rested there, but to Gajapati, she said, 'Pray to the Lord, Gajapati, what is that beneath the tree?'

Diggaj screamed and disappeared. His long legs transported him a mile in virtually an instant.

Bimala knew Gajapati's nature very well; she was sure he would not stop till he had reached the gate to the fort.

Relieved, she proceeded towards the shrine.

But although she had thought of as many eventualities as possible, there was one she had missed. Was the prince even in the temple? Bimala was mortified. She realized that the prince had not promised to be present; all he had said was, 'You can meet me here at this same temple. If you do not see me here, it means we shall not be meeting.' There was thus a possibility of his not being there at all.

And if he was not, all this effort had been in vain. 'Why did I not consider this possibility earlier?' Bimala told herself glumly. 'Why did I have to get rid of Diggaj? How will I return at this hour all by myself? Oh Lord, it is all your will.'

The road to the temple ran past the banyan tree. As she passed the tree, Bimala realized there was nothing beneath it— the white object she had observed earlier was no longer visible. She was a trifle surprised; surely the bull would have been visible in the fields around had it risen and wandered off.

Bimala looked closely at the area under the tree. She thought she spotted someone in a white garment behind the trunk. Quickening her steps, she sped towards the temple, rapping on the door with all her force.

The door was closed. 'Who is it?' a deep voice enquired from within.

'Who is it?' the cry echoed through the empty temple.

'A journey-weary woman,' Bimala answered, summoning all the courage at her disposal.

The door was opened.

Bimala saw a lamp burning within, before it a tall man, his hand on his scabbard. She recognized Prince Jagatsingh.

Chapter Sixteen

In the Lord's Presence

ON ENTERING THE temple, Bimala composed herself and took a seat. She bent head her head in supplication—first to the idol of Shiva, then to the prince. For a few moments, they remained silent, unsure of how to express their minds; both wondered how to begin.

But Bimala was a master of the verbal duel. With a smile, she said, 'The Lord has been kind enough to ensure I have met you, prince. I was frightened while traversing this lonely stretch without a soul for company, but now that I have met you here in this temple, my fear has been dispelled.'

'I trust all goes well with all of you,' responded the prince.

Bimala's intention was to determine, first and foremost, whether the prince was indeed enamoured of Tilottama—all else would come later. With this thought, she declared, 'I am here to offer prayers to Shiva to ensure that all goes well. But now I realize that the Lord is fully satisfied with your prayers and will reject mine, so by your leave, I shall now return.'

Prince: Very well. But you should not travel alone. Allow me to escort you back.

Bimala realized that warfare was not the only art that the prince had acquired mastery over. 'Why would it not be appropriate for me to travel alone?' she asked.

Prince: Many threats lie in wait on the way.

B: Then I shall proceed to King Mansingh at once.

'Why?' asked the prince.

B: Why? I shall complain. The general he has appointed has been unable to keep the land safe for us citizens. He is impotent when it comes to driving the enemy out.

'The general shall respond that exterminating the enemy is impossible even for the gods, never mind humans,' the prince countered with a smile. 'For instance, Shiva himself had reduced his enemy, the god of love, to ashes in the woods; barely a fortnight has passed since then, but that same god is on the rampage again in Shiva's very own temple.'

'Who—is he rampaging against?' Bimala enquired with a laugh.

'Against that very general,' said the prince.

'And why should the king believe such an absurd claim?' asked Bimala.

Prince: I have a witness.

B: Who is this witness, sir?'

Prince: Virtuous lady...

Bimala broke in before he could finish. 'Your servant is most sinful. Please address me as Bimala.'

'Bimala herself is the witness,' declared the prince.

B: Bimala shall not testify thus.

Prince: That is possible, for can a person who can forget her own promise in a fortnight possibly testify truly?

B: What had I promised, sir? Remind me.

Prince: To reveal your companion's identity.

Bimala suddenly abandoned her playful tone, saying gravely, 'I hesitate to reveal her identity, prince. What if it does not please you?'

The prince shed his jocular demeanour too. After a few moments of thought, he said, 'Is there reason for me to be peturbed at by her identity, Bimala?'

'There is,' she answered.

Sinking into a moment's reverie again, the prince said, 'No matter, you must satisfy my curiosity. Nothing can cause greater pain than the unbearable anxiety I have been suffering. Even if your apprehensions are proved correct, that shall be preferable to this agony; I will at least have something to comfort myself with. It is not mere curiosity that has brought me here to meet you, Bimala; at the moment, I do not have the luxury to be curious. For half a month now, I have not slept on a bed other than the back of my horse. I am here only because of my desperation.'

Bimala's efforts had all been in the hope of hearing just such a confession. To hear more, she said, 'You are an expert at politics, prince, do consider, is it right for you in this hour of war to harbour thoughts about a lady out of your reach? I say this for both your sakes, do my companion the favour of forgetting her; I am sure you will triumph in all your battles.'

A rueful smile appeared on the prince's lips. 'Whom do you want me to forget?' he asked. 'Your companion's image has been engraved so deeply in my heart at but a single glance that nothing but the complete destruction of this heart shall erase it. I am known to have a heart of stone; once an image is inscribed in stone, it can only be removed when the stone itself is destroyed. You talk of battle, Bimala? I have been engaged in nothing but battle since I set eyes on your companion— whether on the battlefield or in camp, I have been unable to forget that face for even a moment. When the Pathan raised his sword to cut my head off, all I could think of was that I would never see that face again, that I had seen it but once. Where can I see her again, Bimala?'

Bimala had heard enough. 'You will find her at Fort Mandaran. Tilottama is the daughter of Virendrasingh.'

Jagatsingh felt as though a poisonous snake had sunk its fangs into him. Leaning on his sword, he looked at the floor. After a long while, he sighed deeply, saying, 'You were right. Tilottama can never be mine. I am off to the battlefield; I shall sacrifice my desire for happiness to the enemy's blood.'

Touched by his misery, Bimala said, 'If love were to get its just reward, prince, you deserve Tilottama. But why give up hope altogether? Your fortune may be against you today, but who is to say it will not favour you tomorrow?'

Hope speaks in a sweet tongue. Even in a man's darkest hour, it whispers in his ear, 'No storm lasts forever, why give up? Believe me.' Hope spoke through Bimala, 'Why give up? Listen to me.'

Who can tell what the Almighty desires, Jagatsingh heard hope asking him. Who can read in advance what God has willed? Is there anything in the world that is not possible? Is there anything impossible that has not taken place in this world?

The prince heard words of hope.

'Be that as it may,' he said, 'my agitation knows no bounds; I do not know where my duty lies. Whatever fate holds for me shall come to pass, who can rewrite the will of God? All I can do is to speak my mind. With Shiva as my witness, I swear that I shall never love anyone but Tilottama. My plea to you is to disclose to your companion all that I have told you; and inform her that I only seek her audience one more time, I pledge not to beg for a second meeting.'

Bimala was delighted. 'And how will sir receive my friend's response?'

'I cannot trouble you repeatedly,' answered the prince, 'but if you meet me once more here in this temple, I shall remain grateful to you all my life. One day Jagatsingh shall be of service to you too.'

'Your wish is my command, prince,' said Bimala, 'but I am so afraid to travel by myself all this way at night. I came because I had no choice but to keep my vow. By now this area has been overrun by the enemy, I will be scared to come again.'

After a little thought the prince said, 'If you do not consider that any harm will come of it, I can accompany you

61

to Fort Mandaran. I shall wait somewhere close by, and you can bring me information.'

'Let us go then,' said Bimala happily.

As they were about to leave the temple, soft footsteps were heard outside. 'Has anyone accompanied you here?' the prince asked Bimala in surprise.

'No,' she answered.

'Then whose footsteps were those? I fear someone has been eavesdropping on us.'

But when the prince went out and circled the temple, there was nobody to be seen.

Chapter Seventeen

A Night of Valour

AFTER BOWING BEFORE the deity of Shiva, they left apprehensively for Fort Mandaran. Silence reigned for some time. When they had travelled some distance, the prince was the first to break it. 'I am curious about something, Bimala. I do not know what you will think when you hear what I have to say.'

'What is it?' asked Bimala.

Prince: I am convinced that you are not a maid.

'Why the suspicion?' enquired Bimala with a smile.

Prince: There is a reason why Virendrasingh's daughter may not be the daughter-in-law of the king of Amer. It is a deep secret, how would a mere maid know of it?'

Bimala sighed. 'You have surmised correctly,' she responded a little sadly. 'I am not a maid. Fate has forced me to live the life of one. But why should I blame fate—it has not been unkind to me!'

The prince did not pursue the matter, realizing that the subject had caused Bimala deep regret, The prince did not pursue the matter. 'I *shall* reveal my true identity to you,' Bimala said, unprompted; 'but not now. What is that sound? Is someone behind us?'

Distinct footsteps could now be heard behind them. Two individuals appeared to be whispering to each other. They were a mile from the temple at this time. 'I am sure there is someone behind us,' said the prince. 'Let me check.'

The prince went back along the path they had come, but could see nothing on the road or on either side of it. 'I suspect we are being followed,' he told Bimala on returning. 'It will be wise to keep our voices down.'

They conversed softly as they travelled, eventually arriving at Mandaran village and making their way to the entrance to the fort. 'How will you enter the fort at this hour?' asked the prince. 'The gates must have been closed for the night.'

'Do not worry,' answered Bimala, 'I made sure of that before I left.'

'A secret entrance?' asked the prince, laughing.

'Every thief has one.' Bimala said returning his laugh.

'There is no need for me to go any further,' the prince continued a few moments later. 'I shall wait for you at this mango grove by the fort, please convey my plea frankly to your companion. I shall sleep only after I have seen her one more time, be it a fortnight later or a month.'

'This grove is not secluded, however,' said Bimala. 'You had better come with me.'

Prince: How far should I go?

B: Inside the fort.

'That would not be right, Bimala,' responded the prince after some thought. 'I shall not enter the fort without the permission of its lord.'

'There is nothing to fear,' Bimala assured him.

'We Rajputs do not fear to set foot anywhere,' declared the prince proudly, 'but consider, is it befitting for the son of the king of Amer to enter the fort like a thief without its lord's permission?'

'You shall enter at my behest,' said Bimala.

'Please do not imagine I am slighting you because I think you are nothing but a maid. But tell me, what right do you have to invite me into the fort?'

'You will not enter unless you know my right?' asked Bimala after a pause.

'Never,' came the answer.

Bimala whispered a single word animatedly into the prince's ear.

'Lead on, my lady,' the prince said.

'I am a maid, prince, do not address me as anything but one,' Bimala responded.

'So be it,' said the prince.

The avenue along which Bimala led the prince ended at the entrance to the fort. The mango orchard lay beside the fort, invisible from the main gate. To follow the direction in which the river Amodar flowed behind the women's quarters, one had to pass through the orchard. Bimala now abandoned the high road to enter the orchard with the prince.

Almost instantly they heard the crunch of footsteps on dry leaves.

'Again!' exclaimed Bimala.

'Wait here, while I investigate,' the prince told her.

Drawing his sword from his scabbard, he walked off in the direction of the sound; but he could see nothing. The foliage and wild vines beneath the mango trees was so dense—and the darkness of the shadows cast by the trees so absolute—that he could not see too far ahead. He even wondered whether the sound had in fact been made by grazing cattle rather than human beings. The prince decided not to leave without dispelling his suspicion and climbed a mango tree, his sword in hand. Ascending to the top of the tree, he looked around carefully. After some surveillance, he discovered two figures perched on the branches of a mango tree nearby, all but hidden in the darkness. The moonlight illuminated their turbans, the only part of their bodies which were visible—their faces were concealed by shadows.

Observing carefully, the prince concluded that there was no doubt that there were human beings beneath the turbans. He noted the location of the tree with great care, so as to be able to identify it afterwards. Then, dismounting the tree warily, he returned to Bimala, describing all he had seen, and said, 'If only I had had a spear or two.'

'To what use would you put them?'

Prince: I would have found out who they are. I do not like the indications. From what I can see of their turbans, they are the villainous Pathans, who are pursuing us with some evil motive.

At once Bimala recollected the dead horse by the roadside, the turban, and the hoofprints. 'In that case, wait here, I shall fetch a pair of spears for you from the fort immediately.'

She disappeared in a flash. In the chamber beneath the one in which she had been tending to her hair earlier that evening, a window looked out on the mango orchard. Taking a key from the end of her scarf, Bimala turned it in a secret keyhole, and then pulled the window bars towards herself. By a marvel of craftsmanship, the entire window frame, including the bars, slid into an opening that had appeared in the wall next to it, clearing the way for Bimala to enter. Once she was inside, she tugged on the tiny portion of the window bars that was still visible, whereupon the entire window frame was reinstated in its original position. Bimala reinserted her key in the secret keyhole and turned it to lock the window in place, so that no one could enter.

She went swiftly to the armoury, telling the guard on duty there, 'Do not tell anyone what I am about to ask you for. Give me two spears—I shall return them shortly.'

'What do you want with spears, mistress?' The guard was astounded.

'Tonight is the night one prays for a brave son—and I have to perform special rituals with weapons. Please do not reveal to anyone that I desire to give birth to a son.'

The guard believed her tale, every servant in the fort was under her thumb. Without demur, he handed her a pair of well-honed spears.

Returning to the window swiftly with the spears, Bimala opened it as she had earlier and made her way back to Jagatsingh.

But whether out of carelessness or because of the certainty that she was not going far and would be back soon, Bimala did not secure the entrance through the window behind her when she left. This led to danger. An armed man who had been lying in wait beneath a mango tree very close to the window spotted Bimala's oversight. Keeping himself in the shadow of the tree until she had disappeared from sight, the man shed his noisy leather sandals and tiptoed barefoot up to the window. Peering through the opening to ensure that no one was inside, he took advantage of the breach in the wall to enter.

Meanwhile the prince, armed with the spears supplied by Bimala, mounted the tree again to discover that only one of the two turbans was now visible—the other man was no longer there. Holding one of the spears in his left hand, he aimed at the turban on the branch with the spear in his right hand. Then he threw the spear with all the strength of his powerful arm. There was a loud rustle amidst the leaves in the other tree, followed by the thud of a heavy object falling to ground. The turban could no longer be seen. The prince realized that his infallible aim had felled the owner of the turban.

Dismounting quickly from his tree, the prince raced to the spot where the injured man had fallen. There he saw an armed Pathan soldier lying dead on the ground. The spear was embedded in his head, next to his eye.

Examining the body, the prince realized that the soldier was quite dead. The spear had penetrated his brain. The dead man was carrying a letter in the coat of mail hanging around his neck, a corner of it visible. Extracting it, Jagatsingh read its contents by moonlight:

'Katlu Khan's followers must obey the commands issued by the bearer of this letter as soon as it reaches them. Katlu Khan.'

Bimala had only heard all the sounds, without being aware of what had happened. The prince informed her in detail of all that had taken place. When she had heard the entire account, Bimala said, 'Had I known, I would never have given you the spears, prince. I am a sinner, I shall never be able to atone for the sins I have committed today.

'Why do you regret the death of your enemy? It is right to kill the enemy.'

'Let warriors live by their ethics. We are womenkind.'

'Further delay will cost us dearly,' said Bimala a little later. 'Let us go into the fort, I have kept the way open.'

Arriving soon at the secret entrance, Bimala entered, followed by the prince. As he did, Jagatsingh discovered both his heart and his feet faltering. Why did the warrior who had not turned a hair even in the presence of hundreds of thousands of enemy soldiers now miss a beat of his heart as he was about to enter the abode of joy?

Bimala closed and locked the window as before. Then, taking the prince to her own bedchamber, she said, 'Wait here a short while, I shall be back soon. If you cannot occupy your mind with anything else, consider that God himself sits on nothing but the leaf from a tree.'

Within moments of departing, Bimala was back, opening the door of the adjoining chamber to say, 'Here, prince, I have something to tell you.'

His heart fluttering again, the prince rose to approach Bimala at the doorway to the other room.

Bimala stepped aside at the speed of lightning. The prince saw a fragrant chamber lit by silver lamps, a veiled woman in a corner. Tilottama.

Chapter Eighteen

A Battle of Wits

BIMALA SAT DOWN on her bed. She was elated, for her strategy had been successful. A lamp burnt in the chamber, her mirror lay before her. Her clothes and appearance were as they had been earlier in the evening. She gazed at herself in the mirror for a moment—her hair was still as sinuous, her eyes were still lined with kohl, her lips still tinged with red, her earrings still dangled over her shoulders. Bimala half sat, half reclined against the pillows, smiling at her own reflection. She smiled with vanity—it was not for nothing that the scholar had wanted to abandon his home and hearth for her.

As she waited for Jagatsingh's return, booming war-trumpets were heard in the mango grove. Bimala was startled and afraid too, for war-trumpets were only sounded at the main entrance and never in the orchard. And why at this hour of the night? She recollected all that she had seen and heard that night on her way to and from the temple, realizing that these war-trumpets were a bad omen. Apprehensively, she approached the window, sweeping her eyes over the mango orchard, but could see nothing amiss. She left her chamber anxiously. A courtyard lay directly outside, with another row of chambers on the other side. A wide staircase led up from those chambers to the roof of the palace. Ascending to the roof, she stopped for a moment to look around, but could see nothing in the darkness of the grove. Doubly anxious now, she went up to the parapet of the terrace. Leaning over it, she peered all the way to the base of the fort, but could still see nothing unusual. The green boughs everywhere were flooded by moonlight; they swayed in the gentle breeze from time to time, changing their colour to a yellowish brown. Below, the garden was plunged in almost total darkness, only a few patches of moonlight showing through occasional gaps in the foliage. In the still waters of the Amodar river could be seen reflections of the deep indigo sky with the moon and stars in it. In the distance, on the other shore, was the silhouette of tall buildings, vast towers of the fort, at places the figures of sentries visible on their roofs. Bimala could see nothing more. As she was about to return, her heart despondent, she suddenly felt the touch of a hand on her back. Startled, she turned to see an armed stranger standing behind her. Bimala became as still as a figure in a painting.

'Do not scream,' warned the armed man. 'Screaming is not worthy of a beautiful woman.'

The person who had unexpectedly overwhelmed Bimala was not dressed like an ordinary Pathan solider. His high rank as an officer was evident from the perfection and opulence of his attire. He had not yet crossed thirty; his countenance was exceptionally pleasing. The turban that graced his generous brow was adorned with a single valuable diamond. Had Bimala been calm of mind, she would have realized that he was no less exalted in position than Jagatsingh himself. He may not have been as tall or as broad of shoulders as Jagatsingh, but he was a match for the prince when it came to the stamp of valour and comeliness of appearance, besides being more graceful of build In build, too, he was just as striking. The only weapon he had, besides the unsheathed sword in his hand, was a Damascan knife in a coral sheath attached to his expensive belt.

'Do not shout,' said the warrior. 'It will only bring you harm.'

Ever quick-witted, Bimala regained her composure in a few moments. The armed man's warning had made his motives abundantly clear. Behind her was the edge of the roof, while in front of her was an armed soldier. It would not be difficult for him to push her off the roof. Aware of her predicament, Bimala asked, 'Who are you?'

'How will it benefit you to know?' asked the solider.

'How did you enter the fort?' Bimala asked. 'Have you not been told that thieves are executed?'

Soldier: I am no thief, my beautiful lady.

B: How did you infiltrate the fort?

Soldier: By your grace. I entered while you had kept the window open; I followed you up to the roof.

Bimala chided herself, and then asked again, 'But who are you?'

'Perhaps there is no harm in revealing my identity now,' answered the soldier. 'I am a Pathan.'

B: You are merely revealing your race, not telling me who you are. Who are you?

Soldier: By God's grace, your servant's name is Osman Khan.

B: I do not know any Osman Khan.

Soldier: Osman Khan—Katlu Khan's general.

Bimala began to tremble. She longed to make her escape somehow and warn Virendrasingh. But she had no means to do so, for the general stood before her, barring her way. Left without an alternative, Bimala decided that her freedom would last as long as she could engage him in conversation. Meanwhile, one of the guards in the fort might venture up to the roof. So she resumed the conversation. 'Why are you here?'

'We had sent a messenger to Virendrasingh with a request,' Osman Khan replied. 'He responded, challenging us to storm the fort with our soldiers if we could.'

'So you are here to claim the fort because the lord of the establishment has refused an alliance with you and joined hands with the Mughals,' said Bimala. 'But have you come all by yourself?'

O: For now.

'That is probably why you dare not release me,' said Bimala.

Bimala said this in the hope that the Pathan general might take umbrage at this charge of cowardice and free her.

With a smile, Osman Khan said, 'All one should fear from you, my beautiful lady, is the look you lavish on men. But I do not fear it, I have an appeal to make.'

Bimala looked at him curiously. 'Please oblige me by handing over the keys attached to the end of your scarf,' said Osman Khan. 'I hesitate to offend you with physical contact.'

A woman as intelligent as Bimala did not need time to understand that securing the keys was essential for the general to execute his strategy. She realized, too, that she had no choice, for a request from one who could use force was nothing but a charade. If she did not provide the keys, the general would forcibly seize them from her. Another person would undoubtedly have relinquished the keys at once, but the wily Bimala said, 'How will you seize the keys if I do not hand them over, sir?'

Bimala unwrapped her scarf as she spoke. His eyes trained on it, Osman Khan said, 'If you do not give them to me voluntarily, I shall grant myself the pleasure of touching your body.'

'Then do,' said Bimala, tossing her scarf towards the orchard below. But Osman Khan, who had not taken his eyes off it, reached out to seize the fabric as it floated in the air.

Osman Khan now gripped Bimala's arm tightly, unknotting the fabric with his teeth and transferring the keys to his left hand. His next act left Bimala distraught. Bowing to her several times, Osman said, 'Pardon me,' and used the scarf to tie both her hands firmly to the railing. 'What are you doing?' exclaimed Bimala.

'Tying a love knot,' said Osman.

B: You will shortly face the consequences of this dastardly act.

Osman left. Bimala began to scream, but to no effect. No one heard her.

Descending the same way, Osman returned to the chamber beneath Bimala's. Just as Bimala had done, he inserted the key in the lock and moved the window frame aside. When the opening appeared in the wall, he whistled softly. As soon as he heard it, a soldier appeared on bare feet from behind a tree, and entered the fort. He was followed by another. In this way, a large number of Pathan soldiers infiltrated the fort. To the last person who appeared at the window, Osman said, 'No more, the rest of you can stay outside. Attack the fort when you hear the signal we have agreed to—inform Taj Khan accordingly.'

The soldier returned. Silently, Osman led the band of soldiers inside the fort. As they passed by the roof where Bimala was tied up, he warned them, 'This woman is very clever; do not trust her for a moment. Guard her, Rahim Sheikh; if she tries to escape, or attempts to converse with anyone, or speaks loudly, do not baulk at killing a woman.'

'As you wish,' said Rahim, taking up his position. The Pathan soldiers dispersed across the roof to different parts of the fort.

Chapter Nineteen

Between Lovers

Now that the wily Osman had moved away, Bimala knew she could create an opportunity for escape. Soon, she proceeded to try.

A few minutes after the sentry had taken up his position, she began a conversation with him. Guard on duty or messenger of death, who would willingly spurn a conversation with a beautiful woman? Bimala began with small talk, going on gradually to enquire about the sentry's name and address, his life at home, his joys and sorrows and so on. The guard was pleased at Bimala's interest. Sensing an opportunity, she pulled out all the weapons in her armoury, one by one. The guard melted completely under the assault of Bimala's honey-soaked, flirtatious exchanges, and the suggestive glances from her beautiful eyes. When Bimala realized from his behaviour that he was ready to succumb, she murmured, 'I am scared, Sheikhji. Come sit by my side.'

Smitten, the sentry took a seat next to her. After a few more trivial exchanges, Bimala saw the drug taking effect. The guard kept casting frequent, languishing glances at her. 'You are perspiring so much, Sheikhji. If you untied me, I could fan you. You could tie me up again afterwards.'

There wasn't a single bead of perspiration on Sheikhji's forehead, but why would Bimala say so if there was not? And how many people were fortunate enough to be fanned by her? The sentry untied her at once.

After fanning the guard for some time with her scarf, Bimala draped it around herself again. The sentry did not even bring up the subject of tying her up again. There was a reason for this. Now that she had been untied, the scarf gracing Bimala's body made her appeal shine forth even stronger; the allure that had made Bimala smile at herself in the mirror silenced the sentry altogether.

'Does your wife not love you, Sheikhji?' asked Bimala.

'Why?' he responded in some surprise.

'If she did,' said Bimala, 'why would she stay apart from a husband like you in spring.'

Sheikhji sighed deeply. It was the peak of summer, with monsoon approaching!

Bimala proceeded to fire the arrows in her quiver liberally. 'It is not easy to say this, Sheikhji, but if you were my husband, I would never have let you go to war.'

The guard sighed again. 'If only you were my husband,' Bimala repeated.

Bimala sighed too, throwing him an intense, mysterious look; the guard lost his head. Inching towards Bimala, he edged even closer to her, Bimala also shifted closer to him.

Bimala put her soft hand in the guard's. He was speechless.

'I do not know how to say this,' said Bimala, 'but when you leave after winning the war, will you still remember me?'

G: How could I not remember you?

B: Shall I tell you what I feel?

G: Yes, do.

B: No, I won't, what will you think of me!

G: No, please tell me—think of me as your servant.

B: I have an irresistible urge to leave this sinful husband of mine and run away with you.

That glance again. The sentry wanted to dance with delight.

G: Will you?

The world was full of learned people like Diggaj.

'I will if you will take me,' said Bimala.

G: How could I not take you? I will be your servant.

'How can I reward such love? Accept this from me.'

Unclasping the golden necklace from her neck, Bimala put it around the guard's neck. He promptly ascended to heaven without dying. 'Our scriptures say putting your necklace around another's neck is to marry them,' Bimala continued.

White teeth emerged from the darkness of the guard's beard. 'Then we are married,' he said.

'Of course we are.' Bimala appeared rapt in thought. 'What are you thinking of?' the guard asked.

B: I doubt if fate holds any happiness for me, your army may not conquer the fort.

'There is no doubt about it,' the guard declared with conviction, 'the fort has probably been conquered by now.'

'No, there is a secret,' said Bimala.

'What is it?' said the guard.

B: Let me tell you, so that you can ensure that the fort is indeed conquered.

The sentry waited in anticipation, while Bimala hesitated. 'What is the secret?' the guard asked impatiently.

'What you don't know is that Jagatsingh is waiting beside the fort with ten thousand soldiers. Having learnt that your forces were coming today, he has been lying in wait; he will not strike now, but when your army has let down its guard after conquering the fort, he will surround your soldiers.'

Stunned into silence, the sentry eventually summoned up speech. 'What!'

B: Everyone in the fort knows; we have heard too.

Overcome with joy, the guard said, 'You have made me a wealthy man today, my love! I must inform the general at once, he is certain to reward me for such vital information.'

The sentry had not an iota of suspicion about Bimala.

'You *will* be back, will you not?' said Bimala.

G: Of course I will, in no time at all.

B: You will not forget me?

G: Never.

B: Promise.

'Do not worry,' said the guard, disappearing at a run.

As soon as he was out of sight, Bimala rose to escape too. Osman was right—'It is Bimala's eyes I fear.'

Chapter Twenty

Between Chambers

BIMALA'S FIRST ACT on securing her freedom was to try to inform Virendrasingh. She ran urgently towards his bedchamber.

But before she had covered half the distance, she could hear the Pathans' cries of 'Allah-ho...!'

'Are the Pathans celebrating victory?' Bimala wondered aloud in despair. Soon she could hear a loud commotion —Bimala realized that the inhabitants of the fort had been roused from their sleep. Rushing anxiously towards Virendrasingh's chamber, she heard an uproar there too; the Pathan soldiers had broken through the door. Peeping in, she saw Virendrasingh standing resolutely, sword in hand, bathed in streams of blood. He was swinging his blade like a man possessed, but his charge into battle failed and a blow from a powerful Pathan's long rapier sent his sword flying from his hand. He was taken prisoner.

Thrown into despair by what she had just witnessed, Bimala retreated. There was still time to save Tilottama. She raced off in that direction, only to realize that returning to Tilottama's chamber was well-nigh impossible, for the Pathan soldiers were everywhere. There was no longer any doubt that the Pathans had conquered the fort.

Bimala concluded that she was bound to be captured by the Pathan soliders were she to try to approach Tilottama's chamber. She turned back, disconsolately wondering how she would convey the news of the invasion to Jagatsingh and Tilottama at this hour of crisis. As she stood within a chamber, pondering, she observed a group of Pathan soldiers approaching with the intention of ransacking this room too. In terror, she quickly concealed herself beside an iron safe in a corner. The soldiers arrived and proceeded to loot everything in the chamber. Bimala realized she could not escape, for when the looters would approach the safe to rob what lay within, they were certain to spot her. But taking courage in her hands, she decided to wait awhile, carefully observing what the soldiers were doing. Bimala was infinitely courageous; danger lent her valour a further edge. When she saw the soldiers immersed in their acts of pillage, she emerged with silent footsteps from her hiding spot and made her escape. Completely absorbed in their looting, the soldiers did not notice her. But just as Bimala was about to leave, a soldier crept up from the back and grasped her arm. Turning, Bimala saw it was Rahim Sheikh! 'Where will you go now, runaway woman?'

Bimala turned pale at being held prisoner by Rahim a second time, but only for a moment. She was astute enough to know that she had to appear pleased at seeing him. 'He shall help me get my way,' she told herself. Aloud, she said, 'Shh, come outside, do not let them hear you.'

Taking his hand, Bimala drew him outside, and Rahim followed willingly. Finding themselves alone, Bimala said, 'Shame on you, how could you have left me by myself over there? There is not a place where I have not been looking for you.' She cast that same glance upon him again.

His anger dispelled, Rahim answered, 'I was looking for the general to inform him about Jagatsingh. When I couldn't find him I went looking for you instead, but you were no longer on the roof, so I looked for you all over.'

'When I saw you were not coming, I thought you had forgotten me, and went in search of you,' responded

Bimala. 'What are we waiting for now? Your people have taken possession of the fort, we should seek an escape route immediately.'

'Not tonight, but tomorrow morning,' said Rahim. 'How can I leave without informing them? I shall bid goodbye to the general on the morrow.'

'Then let us get whatever little jewellery I possess, or else one of these soldiers will rob them all.'

'Let us,' said the soldier. Her objective in taking Rahim along as her companion was to ensure that he protected her from other soldiers. Bimala's caution was soon justified. Before they had proceeded much further, they ran into a group of pillaging soldiers. 'Here is a big one,' they burst out on spotting her.

'Mind your own business, brothers,' interjected Rahim, 'do not so much as look this way.'

Sensing his belligerence, the other soldiers relented. 'You are a fortunate man, Rahim,' quipped one of them. 'But pray that the nawab doesn't grab your morsel.'

Rahim and Bimala left. Leading Rahim to the room situated beneath her bedchamber, Bimala said, 'This is my room. Take anything you please. My bedroom is upstairs, I shall be back soon with my jewellery.' Handing him a bunch of keys, she left.

Noting the wealth of riches around the chamber, Rahim happily proceeded to unlock the cupboards and trunks with deep satisfaction. He no longer harboured the slightest mistrust towards Bimala, who had, meanwhile, locked the door from outside and affixed a chain on it, leaving Rahim a prisoner within.

Bimala rushed as fast as she could to her own bedchamber upstairs. The rooms occupied by Tilottama and her were at the extremity of the fort, which the marauding Pathan soldiers had not yet reached—it was doubtful whether Jagatsingh and

80

Tilottama had even heard the tumult. Instead of bursting in on Tilottama, Bimala proceeded to observe her and Jagatsingh secretly through a tiny hole in the door. Old habits die hard —even in the midst of a crisis, Bimala's inquisitiveness knew no bounds! What she saw caused her no small surprise.

Tilottama was sitting on her bed, while Jagatsingh stood near her, surveying her in silence. Tilottama was weeping, while Jagatsingh was wiping his eyes too.

'These are tears of parting, then,' surmised Bimala.

Chapter Twenty-one

Between Swords

'WHAT IS ALL that noise?' asked Jagatsingh when he saw Bimala.

'The Pathans are celebrating victory,' Bimala answered. 'You must find a way out this instant, the enemy will be here any moment.'

'What is Virendrasingh doing?' asked Jagatsingh after a moment's thought.

'He has been captured by the enemy,' Bimala informed him.

A muffled cry escaped Tilottama; she fainted on the bed.

'Look after Tilottama,' the ashen-faced Jagatsingh told Bimala.

Using a rose from a container, Bimala at once sprinkled rosewater on Tilottama's face, neck, and cheeks, fanning her anxiously.

The cries of the enemy grew louder; almost in tears, Bimala said, 'There they come! What will we do now, prince?'

Sparks flew from Jagatsingh's eyes. 'What can I do all by myself?' he said. 'But I can lay down my life to protect your companion.'

The war cries of the enemy came closer still. The clanking of weapons could now be heard, too. 'Tilottama!' screamed Bimala. 'What a time you have chosen to faint. How will I protect you?'

Tilottama opened her eyes. 'Tilottama is conscious again,' declared Bimala. 'Prince! Save her while there is still time, prince!'

'How can she be protected if we remain in here!' said the prince. 'Even now, if the two of you had the strength to leave the room, I might still have been able to escort you out of the fort; but Tilottama cannot move quickly. There, the Pathans are climbing up the stairs, Bimala. I shall be the first to lay down my life, of course, but I regret that even with my own life I shall not be able to save yours.'

In the flash of an eye Bimala swept Tilottama up in her arms. 'Then let us go,' she said, 'I shall carry Tilottama.'

Bimala and Jagatsingh leapt towards the door. Four Pathan soldiers arrived at top speed at the same moment. 'Too late, Bimala,' Jagatsingh said, 'stand behind me.'

Finding themselves face to face with their quarry, the Pathans yelled 'Allah-ho...' cavorting like evil spirits, the weapons at their waist ringing out. But before the cry had been completed Jagatsingh plunged his sword up to the hilt into one of them. The Pathan died, screaming in agony. Before he could withdraw his sword from the slain body, another Pathan aimed his spear at Jagatsingh's neck. Instantly, Jagatsingh's left hand streaked upwards to grasp it, striking a counter-blow with the same spear to hurl its owner to the floor. The very next instant both the remaining Pathans swung their swords at Jagatsingh's head. In the twinkling of an eye the prince severed one enemy soldier's arm, the sword still held in its grip, from his body with a mighty swipe of his own blade, but he could not deflect the blow from the other Pathan. True, the sword did not strike him on his head, but he was dealt a grievous wound on his shoulder. Injured, the prince turned twice as ferocious, like a tiger wounded by the hunter's arrow. No sooner had the Pathan prepared to smite the prince with his weapon again than Jagatsingh, holding his own sword firmly in both his hands, leapt into the air and decapitated the Pathan, whose head, complete with its turban, was split into two. But in the meantime, the soldier whose arm had been severed extracted a dagger from its sheath with his left hand, throwing it at the prince. Even as Jagatsingh was about to resume his footing on the floor after his leap, the dagger sank into his powerful forearm. Brushing it aside like a pinprick, the prince directed a kick at the Yavana's* waist, sending him flying backwards. But just as Jagatsingh was about to decapitate him too, a swarm of Pathans rushed into the chamber, screaming 'Allah-ho...' lustily. The prince realized that to continue the battle would be futile.

Blood flowed all over the prince's body, and he fast grew feeble. Tilottama was still in Bimala's arms, unconscious.

Bimala sobbed as she held Tilottama; her garments were also soaked in the prince's blood.

The chamber filled with Pathan soldiers.

Leaning on his sword, the prince exhaled. 'Abandon your weapon, slave, and we shall spare your life.' The words were like fresh fuel being poured into a fire about to burn itself out. Leaping outwards like a shaft of flame, the prince decapitated the arrogant Pathan who had spoken thus, his head falling at Jagatsingh's feet, swinging his sword, and announcing, 'Watch how a Rajput sacrifices his life, Yavanas.'

The prince's blade flashed like streaks of lightning. When he realized that he could not continue his battle all by himself, he decided to kill as many of the enemy soldiers as he could before dying. With this objective, he positioned himself amidst a phalanx of marauders, gripping his sword with fists of iron and swinging it around his head. He made not the slightest effort to defend himself any more; only showering blows all around. One, two, three—every swing of the sword either felled a Pathan or severed a limb. The enemy's weapons rained blows on the prince from every direction. Now his hands could move no more, blood flowed freely from wounds

---

*Generically any non-Hindu but used here to refer to a Muslim.

all over his body, draining his arm of its strength. His head began to spin, his vision became clouded, and the clamour seemed indistinct to his ears.

'Do not kill the prince, the tiger must be caged alive.'

These were the last words that the prince heard; they had been uttered by Osman Khan.

The prince's arms went limp by his side; the sword fell from his inanimate grip with a clatter on the floor. Losing consciousness, he fell on the corpse of a Pathan soldier he had slain with his own hands. Twenty other Pathans crowded around him to plunder the jewels from his turban. 'Do not touch the prince, any of you,' Osman thundered.

Everyone desisted. With the help of another warrior, Osman Khan hoisted the prince on to the bed. The very same bed which, only a few hours earlier, Jagatsingh had dreamt of sharing with Tilottama after marrying her had now almost turned into his deathbed.

Having placed Jagatsingh on the bed, Osman Khan asked his soldiers, 'Where are the women?'

Osman could not see Bimala or Tilottama anywhere. When the second wave of soldiers had entered the chamber, Bimala had seen the outcome clearly; having no other alternative, she had concealed herself beneath the bed along with Tilottama; no one had observed them.

'Search the entire fort for the women,' commanded Osman Khan. 'The maidservant is very cunning, I will not be at peace if she were to escape. But be careful! Virendra's daughter must not be harmed in any way whatsoever.'

The soldiers dispersed in groups to search different parts of the fort. A few remained to search the chamber. Divining a possibility, one of them cast a light underneath the bed. Spotting his quarry, he announced, 'Here they are.' Osman's face brightened. 'You may come out,' he said, 'without fear.' Bimala emerged first, helping Tilottama out after her. By then

Tilottama had come to her senses—she was able to sit down. 'Where are we?' she asked Bimala softly.

'Cover your face with your veil, do not worry,' Bimala whispered to her.

'Your servant was the one who found them, my lord,' said the soldier who had made the discovery.

'You seek a reward?' said Osman. 'What is your name?'

'Your servant's name is Karim Bux,' came the reply, 'but no one knows me by that name. I was once in the Mughal army, which is why I have been nicknamed the Mughal General.'

Bimala trembled. She remembered Swami Abhiram's prediction.

'Very well, I shall remember,' said Osman Khan.

Part Two

Chapter One

Ayesha

WHEN HE OPENED his eyes, Jagatsingh discovered himself lying on a bedstead in a magnificent palace. It did not appear to him that he had ever been in this chamber before. It was spacious and well-decorated; the floor, cast in stone, was covered with a carpet that felt wondrously soft under the feet. Several rosewater sprinklers and other valuable objets d' art of gold, silver, and ivory were arranged around the room. Blue curtains were draped over the doors and the windows, softening the harsh glare of the sunlight. The chamber was redolent of pleasant aromas.

There was a stillness within, as though no one were present. A single female attendant fanned the prince in silence, sprinkling scented water, while another stood at a distance, as immobile as a wooden puppet devoid of speech. On the ivory-embossed bedstead on which the prince was resting sat a woman, carefully applying a salve to his wounds. On the carpet lining the floor sat an elegantly dressed Pathan, chewing paan and scanning a Persian book. None of them spoke or made any sound.

The prince glanced around the room. He tried to turn on his side, but failed. He felt an acute pain all over his body.

When she observed the prince's efforts, the woman sitting on one side of the bed spoke in a voice as soft as a musical instrument, 'Be still, do not attempt to move.'

'Where am I?' asked the prince in a frail voice.

'Do not attempt to talk, prince, you are in good hands. Do not worry, do not speak.'

'What time is it?' the prince enquired, his voice as frail as earlier.

'It is afternoon,' answered the melodious voice again, softly. 'Be still, you will not recover if you speak. We will leave unless you are silent.'

'One more question, who are you?' asked the prince with great effort.

'Ayesha,' replied the woman.

Silently, the prince glanced at her. Had he seen her earlier? No, he had not, he was convinced.

Ayesha was some twenty-two years of age. She was exquisitely beautiful, but hers was a beauty that is impossible to capture adequately in three or four adjectives. Tilottama was supremely beautiful too, but hers was not Ayesha's kind of loveliness; the eternally young Bimala's beauty used to captivate everyone—but Ayesha's beauty was not like hers either. Some young maidens are lovely like the spring jasmine: freshly bloomed, bashful, tender, pure, fragrant. Tilottama was lovely in this manner. Other women are beautiful like the lily-of-the-field in the late afternoon—its essence on the wane, leaves drying although well-adorned and blooming, overripe, brimming with nectar. Bimala was such a beauty. Ayesha's beauty was like that of a water lily which comes to life under the rays of the morning sun; fully bloomed, fragrant, honeyed, sun-soaked—neither wilted nor drying up, delicate yet radiant. The full petals reflected the sunbeams, yet the smile brimmed over. Have you ever witnessed 'a beauty that lights up the world', reader? Even if you have not, you have certainly heard of it. Many beauties 'brighten up life'. It is said that some people's daughters-in-law become 'the lights of their families' lives'. In the land of Krishna and during Nishumbh's epic battle, even darkness was transformed to light. Has the reader understood by now how beauty can light up the world? Bimala did it too with her beauty, but it was the light of an oil lamp—dimly flickering, of no use without fuel, suitable for domestic tasks. You may use it in your home to prepare your meals and make your bed—anything you want. But touch it, and you will be burnt to death by its flame. Tilottama lit up the world with her beauty too—a light like the glow from a young moon; pure, pleasant, peaceful. But it was not strong enough, and too distant, for domestic tasks. When Ayesha's beauty lit up the world, it was like the rays of the morning sun—brilliant and radiant, yet whatever it lit had no choice but to smile.

As the lotus in the garden, so is Ayesha in this narrative. That is why I desire to paint a clear image of her in the reader's mind. If only I were an artist, so that I could wield a paintbrush to create the perfect shade for her: a colour that is neither burnt sienna, nor crimson, nor ivory, but a mixture of all three. If only I could make that brow as flawless on canvas as it actually is, immaculate and generous, the playground of the god of love; and portray the perfect hairline which borders that forehead. If only I could depict that hairline just as explicitly, following the rounded contours of her forehead to her ears, and make it curve around her ears just as they actually do. If only I could show her hair as black and silky as it is in real life, draw as clear, as fine a parting in her hair as she possesses, colour her hair in its natural hue, give her the same loosely round bun. If only I could recreate those dense black eyebrows, portray how the two eyebrows converge on each other but do not consummate their relationship, how they are appropriately thick at this point but then become slender halfway through their journey, progressively acquiring a fineness as they finish, needle-like by the time they near the hair coiled around the ears. If only I could reproduce those delicate eyelashes, as restless as clouds laden with lightning, represent the largeness of that pair of eyes, the alluring curve of those upper and lower eyelashes, the sapphire tint to her eyes, her bee-black large irises. If only I could display that comely nose with its proudly flaring nostrils, those luscious lips, her alabaster neck revealed by the bun; those full shoulders seeking a touch of the pendants dangling from her ear; her soft, plump, arm bedecked in ornaments; her fingers which dim the lustre of the jewels on her ring; her soft palms tinged with the hue of the pink lotus; her full breasts on which the brilliance of her pearl necklace pales; the enchanting form of her moderately tall body... but even if I could, I would not have picked up the paintbrush. For how would I be able to paint the essence of her loveliness, that precious gem that arises from the churning of oceans, her languid glance—a glance as sweet and languorous as the blue lotus quivering in the evening breeze?

The prince observed Ayesha for a long while. He was reminded of Tilottama. At once his heart seemed to be torn asunder by the memory, the blood rushed in torrents through his veins; deep wounds were reopened. Bleeding profusely, the prince lost consciousness again, his eyes closed.

The lovely woman sitting on the bedstead immediately rose to her feet in fear. The person who was seated on the carpet, reading, had been lavishing loving glances on Ayesha from time to time; when the young woman rose, even the pendants swinging from her ears drew his yearning gaze. Walking slowly up to the Pathan, Ayesha whispered in his ear, 'Summon the physician immediately, Osman.'

It was Osman Khan, conqueror of the fort, who was seated on the carpet. On Ayesha's directions, he rose and left.

Picking up a bowl from a silver stool, Ayesha took a watery substance from it and sprinkled it on the countenance of the unconscious prince.

Osman Khan returned soon with the physician, who staunched the prince's haemorrhaging with great care, and prescribed several different medicines giving instructions in a low tone to Ayesha. 'What is your prognosis?' Ayesha whispered in his ear.

'The fever is perilously high,' answered the physician.

As he was leaving after bidding farewell, Osman followed him to the door to ask softly, 'Will he survive?'

'The signs are ominous,' answered the physician. 'Summon me if he is in pain again.'

Chapter Two

The Stone Within the Flower

AYESHA AND OSMAN stayed by Jagatsingh's bedside late into the night. Jagatsingh hovered between consciousness and oblivion; the physician paid several visits. Ayesha tended to the prince ceaselessly. Well after midnight, a maid arrived to say the Begum had asked for her.

'Coming,' said Ayesha, rising to her feet. Osman also rose. 'Are you going, too?' Ayesha asked him.

'It is late, let me escort you,' said Osman.

Instructing the maids to keep watch, Ayesha proceeded towards her mother's chambers. 'Will you stay with the Begum tonight?' Osman asked her.

'No, I shall return to the prince,' Ayesha answered.

'I cannot praise you enough, Ayesha,' said Osman. 'A sister will not offer to her brother the attention you are offering our arch-foe. You are restoring his life.'

Summoning a smile to her bewitching face, Ayesha said, 'I am a woman, Osman. Tending to the afflicted is my natural calling; not doing it is a sin, but doing it should earn no praise. But what of you? You are the one deserving of praise, for personally supervising, day and night, the treatment and nursing of your enemy—your arch adversary who would rob you of your pride on the battlefield, whom you have personally reduced to this condition.'

'You look upon everyone as a mirror to your own sweet nature,' said a subdued Osman. 'My intentions are not as pure. Do you not realize how much we stand to gain if Jagatsingh survives? How will it benefit us if the prince were to die now? Mansingh is not inferior to Jagatsingh on the battlefield, one warrior will be replaced by another. But if Jagatsingh stays alive, a prisoner in our hands, Mansingh will be compelled to submit to our wishes. To secure freedom for his favourite son, he is sure to conduct a beneficial peace treaty with us. To reclaim a general with such military prowess, Akbar, too, will support such a treaty. And if we can win over Jagatsingh with friendly conduct, he may request, or even atiemp to secure a treaty favourable for us; his efforts will not entirely be in vain. Even if none of these materializes, we will at least secure a rich ransom from Mansingh in return for Jagatsingh's freedom. Jagatsingh's remaining alive will benefit us more than victory over him in open combat.

Osman had undoubtedly directed his efforts towards reviving Jagatsingh because of these reasons; but that was not all. Some people have a propensity for presenting themselves as unyielding individuals, lest they acquire a reputation for kindness; even as they deride compassion as a feminine trait, they come to the aid of other people. If they are asked why, they say it was for their own benefit. Ayesha knew only too well that Osman was such a person. 'May everyone be as farsighted in their selfishness as you, Osman,' she said laughing. 'Ethics will become redundant.'

After some hesitation, Osman murmured, 'I shall provide more evidence of my extreme selfishness.'

Ayesha fixed her eyes, like a cloud charged with lightning, on Osman's face.

'I cling to the vines of hope,' said Osman, 'how much longer must I water its roots?'

Ayesha's countenance turned grave. Osman discerned a new beauty in this transformation, too. 'I spend my time with you as a sister, treating you like my brother. If you step beyond this line, I shall not appear in your presence any more.'

Osman's cheerful expression changed to dejection. 'That same argument forever. Have you imbued this delicate body with a heart of stone, O Lord?'

After escorting Ayesha to her mother's quarters, Osman repaired disconsolately to his own.

And Jagatsingh?

Struck down by high fever, he remained unconscious on his bed.

Chapter Three

Tilottama or You?

THE NEXT MORNING Ayesha, Osman, and the physician were seated as before in Jagatsingh's chamber; Ayesha was on the bed, fanning him with her own hands, the physician was regularly examining his pulse, Jagatsingh was still unconscious. The physician had said that Jagatsingh's critical hour would come that night when the fever was about to leave him; if he could survive it, there would be nothing more to fear. The hour for the fever to drop was at hand, everyone was anxious; the doctor examined his pulse repeatedly, murmuring words like 'weak', 'weaker still', 'a little stronger'. Suddenly his expression changed to one of apprehension. 'It is the hour,' he declared.

Ayesha and Osman remained frozen, listening. The physician held the patient's wrist, feeling for his pulse.

'The indications are poor,' he said a little later. Ayesha looked even more despondent. Suddenly Jagatsingh's face contorted and drained of colour. His fists tightened, his eyes began to roll unnaturally. Ayesha realized the end was almost at hand, death was about to deal its final blow. The physician had been waiting with a vial of potion in his hand, the moment he observed these symptoms he parted the patient's lips and poured it in. Most of the potion trickled down the side of his mouth, but a few drops found their way in. As soon as they did, however, a distinct change manifested itself in the afflicted man. His expression softened gradually, returning his face to its natural form; the unnatural alabaster hue of his skin gave way to a ruddy colour as the blood began to circulate again. His fists fell loose, and his eyes became calm, closing again. The physician examined his pulse with concentration. After a long time, he declared happily, 'He is safe. There is nothing more to be afraid of.'

'Has the fever abated?' enquired Osman.

'It has,' answered the physician.

Both Ayesha and Osman looked pleased. 'There is no further cause for concern,' the physician continued. 'There is no longer any need for me to stay at his bedside. Give him this potion every hour until midnight.' The physician left. Osman repaired to his own chamber after a short while. Ayesha resumed her place on the bed, giving the patient the potion as directed by the physician.

Shortly before the second hour after midnight, the prince opened his eyes. His first sight was of Ayesha's joyful face. The look in his eyes suggested to her that he was not in full possession of his faculties, and that he was striving hard to recollect something, but in vain. After a long interval, he looked at Ayesha to ask, 'Where am I?' These were the first words uttered by the prince in two days.

'In Katlu Khan's fort,' answered Ayesha.

Once again the prince tried to gather his memories. 'Why am I here?' he asked after another long interval.

Ayesha did not answer at first. Eventually, she said, 'You are ailing.'

The prince thought about this and shook his head. 'No, I have been captured,' he said.

His expression changed as he said these words.

Ayesha did not answer; she could see that the prince's memory was being rekindled. 'Who are you?' the prince asked again after a few moments.

'I am Ayesha.'

'Who is Ayesha?'

98

'Katlu Khan's daughter.'

The prince fell silent again; he lacked the strength for a long conversation. 'How long have I been here?' he asked after a short rest.

'Four days.'

'Is Fort Mandaran still under the control of your forces?'

'It is.'

After another short rest, Jagatsingh continued. 'And what was Virendrasingh's fate?'

'He has been imprisoned, he will be tried today.'

Jagatsingh's expression grew even more dejected. 'What is the condition of the other citizens?'

Ayesha was alarmed. 'I do not know everything,' she answered.

The prince said something to himself. A single name escaped his throat, which Ayesha could hear. 'Tilottama.'

Ayesha rose slowly to fetch the delicious potion prescribed by the physician; the prince surveyed her beautiful form, his eyes coming to rest on the pendants swinging from her ears. After drinking the potion Ayesha had brought him, he said, 'When I was ill, I dreamt I was being tended to by an angel from heaven. Was it you, or was it Tilottama?'

'You must have been dreaming of Tilottama,' responded Ayesha.

Chapter Four

The Woman Behind the Veil

LATE ONE MORNING, TWO days* after conquering the fort, Katlu Khan held his court. His courtiers were arrayed in two rows on either side of him, while several thousand people were seated on the floor before the throne. Virendrasingh was to be sentenced.

Several armed guards brought Virendrasingh, bound in chains, to the court. His countenance was bloodshot, but it held no sign of fear. His glittering eyes appeared to be emitting sparks, his quivering nostrils were flared, he kept biting his lips. When he was presented before Katlu Khan, the Nawab said, 'Virendrasingh! I shall now sentence you for your crime. Why did you choose to antagonize me?'

Virendrasingh's face had darkened with rage; controlling himself, he said, 'Before that I insist on knowing what act of antagonism I have committed.'

'Speak with a civil tongue,' warned a courtier.

'Why did you refuse me the troops and money I had demanded?' asked Katlu Khan.

'You are a bandit who has rebelled against the king,' Virendrasingh declared fearlessly. 'Why should I send you soldiers? Why should I send you money?'

The spectators realized that Virendrasingh had embarked on a suicidal course.

---

* It should be actually four days after the conquest. The author most likely made a small error.

Katlu Khan's enormous frame trembled with rage. But having mastered the art of containing his anger, he spoke calmly, 'Why did you ally with the Mughals while residing in my kingdom?'

'By what right is it your kingdom?'

Even more enraged, Katlu Khan said, 'Listen to me, you miserable cur! You shall now pay for your offences. Until this moment, there was some hope of saving your life, but you are foolish, you are hastening your own execution with your bluster.'

Laughing arrogantly, Virendrasingh said, 'Since I have been brought to you in chains, Katlu Khan, I do not expect mercy. Of what value is life to one who is allowed to live by an enemy such as yourself? I would have blessed you before I died—but you have besmirched my lineage, because of you my most precious possession, dearer than life itself…'

Virendrasingh could speak no more; his voice choked, his eyes brimmed with tears. The intrepid, arrogant Virendrasingh began to weep, his eyes lowered.

Katlu Khan was cruel by nature, so vindictive that the suffering of others elated him. His expression brightened at the sight of his bold adversary thus reduced to tears. 'Are you not going to appeal for my clemency, Virendrasingh?' he said. 'Consider, for your time is nigh.'

His tears helped abate the agony in Virendrasingh's heart. Speaking with greater composure than before, he said, 'I ask for nothing else other than that my execution be conducted summarily.'

K: So it shall be. Anything else?

V: Not in this lifetime.

K: You do not wish to meet your daughter before you die?

The spectators were quiet with remorse at this question, while Virendra's eyes began to blaze again.

'If my daughter is alive in your residence, I do not wish to meet her. If she has died, bring her, I shall die with her in my arms.'

The spectators remained silent. So silent was the huge gathering that a pin would have been heard dropping. At a signal from the Nawab, Virendrasingh was led to the execution ground. Before he reached, however, a Muslim man whispered something in his ear, of which Virendra could understand nothing. He handed Virendra a letter. Opening it distractedly, he discovered it was written in Bimala's hand. Crumpling it in his fist, he hurled it away with great fury. Retrieving the letter, its bearer withdrew. 'Is it a letter from his daughter?' one of the spectators who had witnessed this act asked another softly.

Virendra heard him. Turning, he said, 'Who says it is from my daughter? I have no daughter.'

Before leaving with the letter, its bearer told the guards, 'Delay the execution till my return.'

'As you command, sir,' chorused the guards.

The bearer of the letter was none other than Osman, which was why the guards addressed him with respect.

Osman entered the inner chambers of the palace, where a veiled woman awaited him behind a tree. Osman went up to her and, ensuring that no one could overhear them, related all that had happened. The veiled woman said, 'I have put you to a great deal of trouble, but we have arrived at our present condition because of you. No one but you can accomplish this task for me.'

Osman did not speak.

The woman behind the veil continued, her voice breaking with despair. 'If you do not wish to, do not aid us. We may be helpless today, but there is a God!'

'You do not know, my lady, how difficult a task you have set me. Should he be informed, Katlu Khan will condemn me to death.'

'Katlu Khan?' said the lady. 'Why do you wish to delude me? Katlu Khan dare not touch a hair of yours.'

You do not know Katlu Khan—but come, let me take you to the execution ground.

The veiled woman followed Osman and stood in the execution ground in silence. Virendrasingh did not observe her, for he was deep in conversation with a Brahmin dressed as a mendicant. Peering through her veil, the woman saw it was Swami Abhiram.

'Permit me to take my leave, my lord,' Virendra said to Swami Abhiram. 'What can I possibly tell you before I go? I have no wish to make in this world, whom should I make a wish for?'

Swami Abhiram indicated the woman in the veil standing behind Virendrasingh. When he turned to look at her, the woman threw aside her veil and flung herself at Virendra's chained feet. 'Bimala!' he cried passionately.

'My husband! My lord! My dearest one!' Speaking like one not in her senses, Bimala said even more loudly, 'I shall reveal all to the world today, who can force me to desist? My husband! Jewel of my life! Where do you go? Where do you leave us?'

Virendrasingh's eyes streamed with tears. Taking her hand, he said, 'Bimala, my love! Why must you make me weep now, the enemy will think I am afraid.'

Bimala fell silent. 'Let me go, Bimala,' Virendra continued. 'You can follow me.'

'We will,' responded Bimala. 'We will, but not before avenging this suffering,' she added sotto voce.

Virendrasingh's countenance brightened, like a lamp flaring before it is snuffed out. 'Will you be able to?' he asked.

Pointing to her right hand, Bimala said, 'With this hand. I hereby forsake the gold on this hand now, what need have I

103

for it any more.' Flinging away her bangles, she said, 'The only ornament in this hand will now be of sharpened iron.'

'You will be able to,' said Virendrasingh with satisfaction, 'may God fulfil your wish.'

'I cannot wait any more,' called the executioner.

'This is it. Go now,' Virendra told Bimala.

'No, let my widowhood occur in my presence,' said Bimala. 'Your blood shall overcome my fears.' Her voice was ominously calm.

'So be it,' said Virendrasingh, signalling to the executioner. Bimala saw his upraised axe glint in the sunlight; her lashes lowered themselves without her bidding. When she opened them again, she saw Virendrasingh's severed head, bathed in blood, rolling on the ground.

Bimala stood frozen like a statue, without a single hair on her head moving in the breeze. Not a teardrop escaped her eyes. She could not look away from the severed head.

Chapter Five

The Widow

WHERE WAS TILOTTAMA? Where was the fatherless, orphaned child? Where, for that matter, was Bimala? How had Bimala appeared at the site of the execution? And where did she vanish afterwards?

Why had Virendrasingh not sought a final meeting with his beloved daughter before his death? Why, indeed, had he become inflamed with anger at the mention of her name? Why had he declared, 'I have no daughter'?

Why had he flung away Bimala's missive without perusing it?

Why? Recollect how Virendrasingh had berated Katlu Khan, and you will be seized of the dreadful events that had occurred.

'The unsullied reputation of our clan has been besmirched,' the chained tiger had roared.

The question is, O reader, where were Tilottama and Bimala? Look for them in the chambers occupied by Katlu Khan's concubines—you shall find them there.

Such are the turns that life takes. In such a merciless manner does the wheel of destiny grind. Beauty, youth, innocence, chastity—all of them are crushed under the rim of this giant wheel.

It was Katlu Khan's habit was to acquire for his personal harem any uncommonly beautiful woman taken prisoner at a village or fort by his army. As was the practice, he had arrived at Fort Mandaran on the day after its fall to inspect the arrangements made for prisoners, and to deploy soldiers for defending the fort. As soon as he had set eyes on Bimala and Tilottama amongst the prisoners, he had issued instructions for them to be taken away to adorn his palace of pleasures. He had subsequently found himself deeply engaged in other matters of importance. Having heard that Rajput soldiers were preparing an assault in retaliation against Jagatingh's imprisonment, he had diverted his attentions to plotting their defeat—and had not, therefore, had the leisure to enjoy the company of his new handmaidens.

Bimala and Tilotttama had been installed in separate chambers. There on the floor, reader, lay the dust-smeared form of the fatherless young woman. There is no gain to be had in bestowing a look upon her. What use can it be? Who is willing to lavish even a single glance on Tilottama any more? At the advent of spring, when fresh vines sway in a gentle breeze, is there anyone who will not be drawn by their fragrance to stay awhile beside them? And when it falls to the earth, uprooted— along with the tree in whose shelter it had grown—by a summer thunderstorm, is there anyone who spares a look for it concealed amidst the remains of the fallen tree? Woodmen chop up the tree for its timber, while the vines are only crushed underfoot

Let us abandon Tilottama and go elsewhere. Let us go where, instead of the lively, resourceful, witty, Bimala—lover of the joys of life—sits a grave, repentant, melancholy widow, her eyes covered with the end of her saree.

Is this indeed Bimala? Gone are her braids, her hair is matted. Her embroidered scarf has disappeared, as has her jewel-encrusted blouse. Her garments are soiled, tattered, and austere. Where are her splendid ornaments gone? Where are the earrings that once yearned to caress her shoulders? Why are her eyes swollen? Where have those glances gone? Why does her forehead sport a wound? Look, it is bleeding!

Bimala was waiting for Osman.

Osman was the pride of the Pathans. War was his profession, his personal calling, his creed; so he baulked at nothing in order to win. But once Osman had triumphed on the battlefield, he never permitted the vanquished to be tortured needlessly. Had Katlu Khan himself not pronounced his dreadful sentence, Osman would not have allowed Bimala and Tilottama to remain prisoners. It was because of his benevolence that Bimala had been allowed an audience with her husband at his hour of death. When Osman later learnt that Virendrasingh was Bimala's husband, his compassion deepened further. Because he was Katlu Khan's nephew, he was free to go anywhere he wished within the palace, as we have observed already. True, the wing of the palace in which Katlu Khan's concubines lived was out of bounds even for his sons, as it was for Osman. But he was Katlu Khan's right-hand man, whose prowess had enabled the nawab to conquer Utkal all the way up to the banks of the Amodar river. Thus the denizens of the palace were almost as subservient to Osman as they were to Katlu Khan himself. That was how Bimala's prayer to meet her husband at his final hour come to be granted.

Two days after she had become a widow, Bimala handed over whatever jewelry she still had in her possession to the maid assigned to her. 'What are your instructions for me?' asked the maid.

'Go to Osman once again, as you did the other day,' Bimala told her. 'Tell him that I request an audience with him once more; inform him that this is the last time, I shall not seek another one.'

The maid performed her bidding. 'To visit her quarters would put both of us in jeopardy,' Osman responded. 'Request her to visit my chamber.'

'How can I possibly do such a thing?' asked Bimala.

'He has said he will make arrangements,' the maid replied.

When evening fell, a maid of Ayesha appeared. After talking with the sentries at the door, she took Bimala to Osman.

'In what way may I be of service?' enquired Osman.

'A small matter,' said Bimala. 'Is Prince Jagatsingh alive?'

O: He is.

B: Is he free or imprisoned?

O: He is indeed a prisoner, but not in prison at present. He is confined to bed, afflicted by wounds. I have kept him here within the palace without Katlu Khan's knowledge, for that is how he can be tended to with special attention.'

'It is we accursed women who have brought ill-luck upon the prince. It is all the will of God. If the prince recovers, pray give him this letter after his recovery. Until then, keep it with yourself. This is my only plea.'

Returning the missive, Osman said, 'It would not be right of me; no matter what condition the prince is in, he is considered a prisoner. It is against the law to give a letter to a prisoner without having read it first, and would mean flouting my lord's orders.'

'This letter contains nothing that can cause you or your people any harm; you shall not be flouting the law, therefore. And as for your lord's orders, are you not your own lord?'

'In some matters I may choose to defy my elders, but the present instance is not among them. Since you state that there is nothing against us in this letter, I am convinced it is so. But I cannot break the law in such a matter. I regret that I am unable to comply with your bidding.'

'Then you may read it before you hand it over to the prince,' said Bimala, disappointed.

Accepting the missive, Osman began to read it.

Chapter Six

Bimala's Letter

'O PRINCE! I had vowed to reveal my true identity to you one day. That day is here.

'I had trusted that my Tilottama would be crowned the queen of the state of Amer before I made my identity known. All those hopes have been extinguished. I believe you shall shortly be informed that there is neither a Tilottama nor a Bimala in this world any more. Our days are drawing to a close.

'That is why I write this letter to you now. I am a despicable sinner, I have transgressed repeatedly, people will condemn me after my death, and many execrable things shall be said about me. Who then will attempt to wipe the stain off my reviled name? Do I have such a well-wisher in this world?

'There is one, however. He will shortly leave civilization to retreat into meditation. Swami Abhiram will not, therefore, serve the purpose for this forsaken woman. I had imagined, even if for a day, prince, that one day I would be counted among your family. Today, then, do for me what you would do for someone in your family. But whom am I making this entreaty to? Such is the fortune of this ill-fated woman that it has, like a flame, seared even the ally who had stood by her side. Be that as it may, forget not my petition. When people say Bimala brought disgrace to her clan, that Bimala was a harlot in the guise of a maid, please tell them that Bimala was born into a low caste, that Bimala's fate was wretched, that she was guilty of a hundred sins wrought by a poorly controlled tongue; but Bimala was not a harlot. He who has now ascended to heaven had, by Bimala's good fortune, accepted her hand with all due rituals. Not for a day was Bimala unfaithful to her lord.

'When none of this was known all this time, who will believe it now? Listen now to why I lived the life of a maid although I was a wife.

'A man named Shashishekhar Bhattacharya once resided in a village near Fort Mandaran. The son of an affluent Brahmin, he was given an education just like everyone else in his clan. But education cannot eradicate blemishes in character. Although God had bestowed every quality on Shashishekhar, he had also given him one terrible flaw, the flaw that all young men suffer from.

'In the family of one of the followers of Jaidharsingh in Fort Mandaran lived a woman whose husband was far away. She was exceptionally beautiful. Her husband, who was a soldier in the king's army, had for long been away in a distant land. This beautiful woman became the object of Shashishekhar's wanton desires—soon his seed had impregnated the woman.

'Neither fire nor sin can be concealed very long. Shashishekhar's misdeed soon came to his father's notice. To mitigate the calumny that his son had heaped upon another's family, Shashishekhar's father had the woman's husband brought back home at once, and admonished his errant son roundly. His reputation ruined, Shashishekhar left home.

'Leaving his family residence, he travelled to Kashi, where he began to study with a renowned ascetic whose learning he had heard about. Being well endowed with intelligence, he became extremely proficient in philosophy and unmatched in astrology. His tutor was extremely pleased with his pupil.

'Shashishekhar used to reside near the house of a Shudra woman, who had a daughter recently come of age. Out

110

of respect for the Brahmin, the daughter performed all his domestic tasks, which included serving his meals. It is one's duty to shed the burden of one's parents' misdeeds. It is unnecessary to say more , Shashishekhar's seed led to the birth of this unfortunate creature from the Shudra girl's womb.

'As soon as he heard of this, the scholar said, 'Sinners are not permitted to study with me, my son. Do not show yourself in Kashi ever again.'

'Shamed, Shashishekhar left Kashi.

'My grandmother evicted my mother from her home on grounds of promiscuity.

'My luckless mother took up her abode with me in a hut, sustaining herself through physical labour. No one spared her a second glance. There was no news of my father, either. Some years later, in winter, a wealthy Pathan was passing through Kashi on his way to Delhi from Bengal, accompanied by his wife and newborn son. He had nowhere to spend the night, having arrived in the city late in the evening. Finding themselves by my mother's dilapidated cottage, they sought to spend the night there, saying, "No one in the Hindu neighbourhood will let us in at this hour. Where can we go with this little boy? He will not survive the cold outdoors. There are only a few of us, and your cottage will accommodate us comfortably. I will reward you handsomely." In truth the Pathan was in a hurry to get to Delhi for a particular reason, and the family was accompanied by only one manservant. My mother was poor, but also compassionate. Whether out of greed or out of kindness for the child, she allowed the Pathans to occupy the hut that night. Along with his wife and son, the Pathan slept in one part of the cottage, a lamp lit by their side, while we slept in the other part.

'There was a fear of kidnappers in Kashi at the time. I was only a girl of six, I cannot recollect all of it and am now recounting what I heard from my mother.

111

'The lamp was lit, a thief had stolen into the hut and was about to abduct the Pathan's son, when I woke up suddenly. I saw what the intruder was doing, and seeing him drag the child away, cried out loudly, waking everyone.

'The Pathan's wife realized her son was not in his bed. She screamed. The kidnapper had concealed himself beneath the cot with the child. Dragging him out by his hair, the Pathan snatched his son back from the intruder's grasp. Indulging his tearful appeals for mercy, the Pathan only sliced off his ears with his sword and released him.'

Having read the letter thus far, Osman asked Bimala, his mind distracted, 'Did you not have a different name once?'

'I did. My father changed it because it was a Yavana name.'

'What was the name? Was it Mehroo?'

'How did you know?' asked Bimala in surprise.

'I am that boy who was almost kidnapped,' answered Osman.

Bimala was astonished. Osman continued reading.

'As they were leaving the next morning, the Pathan said, "I do not have the means to repay your daughter for what she has done for us. But if you wish for some particular object, tell me. I am going to Delhi, I shall send you the object of your desire from there. If it is money you need, I shall send that too."

'"I do not desire wealth," said my mother. "I support my daughter and myself comfortably with my labour, but if you do have some influence with the emperor…"

'"I have a great deal of it," the Pathan interjected. "I can do something for you at the royal court if you wish me to."

'"Then pray enquire after the whereabouts of the father of this girl and inform me," said my mother.

'The Pathan promised to do so and left. To my mother he offered gold coins, which she did not accept. As he had vowed to, the Pathan engaged individuals at the royal court to look for my father; but he could not be found.

'Fourteen years later, however, they finally found my father and sent a letter to my mother. He was in Delhi, living under the name of Swami Abhirama, having forsaken his original identity of Shashishekhar Bhattacharya. But by the time the news arrived, my mother had passed away. If one who has been married without religious rites can be admitted to heaven, there is no doubt that my mother ascended nowhere else.

'Once I had received news of my father, I found myself unable to remain in Kashi. With my father being the only living member of my family, why live in Kashi when he was in Delhi? With this thought, I travelled alone to meet him. At first my father was angry at my arrival, but when I pleaded tearfully with him, he eventually relented, permitting me to live with him and serve him. He changed my name from Mehroo to Bimala. In my father's home I devoted myself to taking care of him, putting all my heart into satisfying him. I did it not to serve some purpose of my own or to win his affection—serving my father did in fact give me immense joy. I had no one but him. I used to consider the privilege of serving one's father the greatest happiness of all. As for my father, whether it was because of my devotion to him or because of the natural instinct of the heart, he too began to lavish his affection on me. Love is like a river that flows to the sea—the further it progresses, the more it widens. When my period of happiness finally ended, I discovered how much my father had loved me.'

113

Chapter Seven

The End of Bimala's Letter

'I HAVE ALREADY mentioned that an impoverished woman in Fort Mandaran had also been impregnated by my father's seed. Her destiny proved to be the same as her mother's. The fruit of her womb, too, was a daughter, and when the young girl's mother was widowed unexpectedly, like my mother, she too resorted to physical labour to earn a living and support her daughter. The Lord has ruled that gold can emerge from dross. Even an unyielding mountain can bring forth tender, soft flowers; the brightest gems glow in the depths of the darkest mines. A wondrously beautiful daughter was born in that impoverished home. The widow's daughter acquired a reputation as a woman of rare beauty in Fort Mandaran. Time obliterates everything, time obliterated the widow's stigma, too. Many people forgot that her beautiful daughter had been born out of wedlock; some did not know it at all. Within the fort, almost no one was aware of it. Why go further? This beautiful woman was married and gave birth to Tilottama.

'It was this marriage that brought about the most important event in my life, which took place while Tilottama was in her mother's womb. One day my father arrived home accompanied by his son-in-law. He introduced the stranger to me as his disciple, but my departed lord revealed his real identity to me.

'From the moment I set eyes on him, my heart belonged to him. But how can I possibly reveal all that? Virendrasingh realized I would never be his except through marriage. My father's intuition told him everything. One day, I overheard their conversation on the subject.

'"I cannot live without Bimala," declared my father. "But if she were to become your wedded wife, I shall live with both of you. If, however, that is not your intention…"

'Before he could finish, my departed husband said angrily, '"How can I marry the daughter of a Shudra woman, my lord?"

'"How did you bring yourself to marry a woman born out of wedlock?" my father asked sarcastically.

'"When I married her I did not know she was born out of wedlock," said my dearest one in disappointment. "But how can I knowingly marry a Shudra woman? And your elder daughter may have been born out of wedlock, but she is not a Shudra."

'"You have refused to marry her. So be it. Your visits here will cause harm to Bimala. There is no need for you to come to me any more, I shall meet you at your residence."

'After that, he stopped visiting our home regularly, as he was wont to. I waited impatiently for him every day; my hopes were belied for a period of time. But soon, I imagine, he could contain himself no longer, and resumed his visits. Now that I began to meet him once again, I was bashful no longer. Observing this, my father summoned me one day. "I will embrace the life of a peripatetic monk, I shall be unable to live with you permanently. Where do you propose to stay when I am on my journeys?"

'Miserable at the prospect of being separated from my father, I began to cry. "I shall go with you," I declared. "Alternatively, I shall live by myself here, as I used to in Kashi."

'"No, Bimala," my father told me. "I have arrived at a far wiser decision. I shall appoint a suitable protector for you in my absence. You shall be engaged in providing company to King Mansingh's newest queen."

'"Do not abandon me," I pleaded with him tearfully. "No, I shall not go anywhere," my father said. "Go to Mansingh's palace. I shall remain here, and visit you every day. Your sojourn there will enable me to determine my future course of action."

'And so I joined the serving women in your abode, prince. My father craftily removed me to a place where I was beyond his son-in-law's reach.

'I remained among the chambermaids in your residence for a long time, prince; but you do not know me. For you were only a boy of ten then; you lived with your mother in the royal palace of Amer, while I was engaged in serving your (newlywed) stepmother in Delhi. Like a garland of blossoms, innumerable women were to be found encircling King Mansingh's neck; did you even know all your stepmothers? Can you recollect Urmila Devi, who originated from Jodhpur? How can I describe to you her many qualities? She considered me not her attendant maid but her very own sister, dearer to her than her own heart. She accorded me a certain status, and painstakingly taught me many skills. It was by her grace that I acquired various arts. It was to entertain her that I learnt singing and dancing. She personally taught me how to read and write. That I have been able to write this letter to you— albeit in my poor script—is by the grace of your stepmother Urmila Devi.

'My friend Urmila's generosity proved beneficial in another important manner. She presented me to the king with the same affection with which she treated me. I had developed some aptitude for singing, and listening to me sing was a pleasurable experience for the king too. Whatever be the reason, King Mansingh considered me part of his family. He used to revere my father, who visited me frequently.

'I was happy in every way in Urmila Devi's company. My only regret was that I caught not a glimpse of the person for

116

whom I was willing to forsake everything except my religion. Had he forgotten me, then? It was not so. Do you remember the chambermaid named Aasmani, prince? Perhaps you do. Aasmani and I developed a particular attachment. I requested her to procure news of my lord. Making enquiries, she gave him news about me as well. How do I tell you all the things he wrote to me in response. I sent him a letter through Aasmani, he wrote back too. These exchanges continued repeatedly. Although we did not meet, we continued conversing.

'Three years passed thus. When we realized that neither had forgotten the other in spite of those years of separation, we knew that our love was not ephemeral like the moss floating on the surface of the water; it was deep-rooted like the lotus. I do not know why, but his patience was exhausted by now. One day he decided to change everything. I was alone in my chamber, asleep in my bed. Awaking suddenly, in the dim lamplight I discovered someone standing nearby.

"Do not be afraid, beloved. I am your very own servant." I heard these magical words addressed to me.

'What would I say in response? We were meeting after three years. I forgot what I wanted to say—all I could do was fall into his arms and weep. I will die shortly and thus I am not ashamed today to disclose everything.

'When I regained my power of speech, I asked, "How did you enter?"

"Ask Aasmani," he replied. "Disguised as a servant bearing water, I accompanied her into the palace. I have been in concealment since then."

'"And now?" I asked.

'"I am in your hands," he said.

'I wondered what I should do, what choice I should make. My impulse was to follow my heart. As these thoughts ran through my mind, the door to my bedchamber was flung open. King Mansingh stood before me.

117

'Details are unnecessary. Virendrasingh was imprisoned. The king intended to sentence him by the royal code. Possibly he understood what was going on in my heart. I surrendered in tears at Urmila Devi's feet, admitted all my transgressions, and accepted the entire responsibility. When I met my father, I surrendered at his feet too. The king venerated him, held him in the highest esteem as his spiritual teacher—he was certain to honour his request. "Remember your eldest daughter," I told him. I believe my father was in league with the king. He paid no heed to my tears. "Sinner!" he said angrily. "You have no shame."

'Urmila Devi made many petitions to the king to spare my life, whereupon the king said, "I shall release the intruder provided he marries Bimala."

'Grasping the king's intentions, I remained silent. Enraged at this demand, my beloved said, "I would rather stay incarcerated all my life. I would rather be executed. But I will never marry the daughter of a Shudra. How can you be a Hindu and make such a request?"

'"When I have given my sister in marriage to Prince Salim, why should it be surprising that I am requesting you to marry a Brahmin's daughter?"

'Still he was not willing. "Whatever has happened is over and done with," he said instead. "Grant me my freedom, I shall never utter Bimala's name again."

'"Then how will you atone for your crime?" said the king. "If you abandon Bimala, others will revile her for having a stain on her character and will not touch her."

'Despite all this there was no immediate agreement to marriage on his part. Eventually, when he could endure the torture of imprisonment no longer, he half-agreed, saying, 'If Bimala can live in my household as a maid, if she never refers to the marriage in her life, if she never identifies herself as my wedded wife, only then shall I marry a Shudra's daughter—not otherwise."

'Elated, I agreed to all his conditions. I was not desirous for wealth, glory, or status. Both my father and the king gave their assent. I left the king's palace and entered my consort's in the guise of a maid.

He had married me unwillingly, under pressure applied by powerful people. Who can make love to a wife whom he has married in such circumstances? After our wedding my lord began to abhor the very sight of me. His earlier love for me disappeared. Recollecting the humiliation heaped upon him by King Mansingh, he rebuked me constantly, but even his harsh words appeared like lovemaking to me. Some time had passed this way; but why go into all that? I have revealed my identity, nothing more is required. In time I regained my husband's affections, but his hostility towards the king of Amer did not dissipate. It is all part of destiny. Why else should all this have happened?

'And thus I have revealed my identity to you. Honouring my vow is not my only intention. Many people believe I betrayed the honour of my family to live with the lord of Fort Mandaran. It is with the hope that you will clear my name of the calumny heaped on it that I write this to you.

'I have only written about myself in this letter. I have not even referred to the one whose news you are anxious to hear. Consider her name wiped off the face of this earth. Forget that there ever was one named Tilottama…'

When he had finished reading, Osman said, 'You saved my life once, my lady, I shall repay you.'

'What can I possibly need in this world any more?' Bimala sighed. 'What can you do for me? There *is* something, however…'

'Tell me and I shall do it,' said Osman.

Bimala's eyes brightened. 'What are you saying, Osman? Must you deceive this broken heart?'

119

'Accept this ring,' said Osman, taking off one of his rings. 'We cannot do anything in the next day or two. But Katlu Khan's birthday is almost upon us, it is a day of raucous celebrations. The guards lose themselves in all the pleasures on offer. I shall rescue you that day. Appear at the door to the women's chambers that night; if someone displays a ring identical to this one, come out with him. I trust that you shall be able to escape unscathed. Of course, it is all God's will.'

'May God grant you a long life, what more can I wish for you,' said Bimala. Her voice choked, she could talk no more.

As she was about to leave after casting her benedictions on Osman, he said, 'I must warn you about something. Pray come alone. If you have a companion, the task shall not be accomplished—on the contrary, there will be danger.'

Bimala realized that Osman was forbidding her to bring Tilottama. 'Very well,' she reflected, 'if both of us cannot go, Tilottama will go alone.'

Bimala left.

Chapter Eight

Recovery

THE DAYS PASSED. Do as you please, the days will pass, not pause. Live in the manner that you please, the days will pass, not pause. Do you find yourself stranded in unexpected, torrential rain, traveller? Do the clouds thunder loudly overhead? Are you soaked by the downpour? Is your unprotected body buffeted by hail? You cannot find shelter? Be patient but awhile— this day too shall pass, it will not last. Wait but awhile, the adverse period will pass, a favourable cycle will begin. The sun will rise, but you must wait till tomorrow.

Is there anyone for whom the days do not pass? Is there anyone whose sorrows are made permanent by time standing still? Why then do you weep?

Who is it for whom time stands still? Tilottama languished on the floor, but still the days passed.

The serpent of vengeance had made the flower of Bimala's heart its home, infecting her body with its poison, its sting unbearable for even a moment, let alone all the moments that constitute an entire day. And yet, did the days not pass?

The conqueror of enemies, Katlu Khan, occupied the throne; his days passed happily. The days passed, they did not pause.

Jagatsingh was ailing; who does not know how long each day in an ailing man's life seems? And yet the days passed.

The days passed. Jagatsingh recovered a little every day. Having secured a reprieve from a death sentence, the prince was less and less in danger with every passing day. First his discomfort ceased; then his appetite returned, followed by strength of body, and then by anxiety.

His first question—where was Tilottama? The faster he recovered, the more he asked everyone with mounting desperation, but no one could provide a satisfactory answer. Ayesha did not know, Osman would not say; the servants and maids were not aware either, or were instructed not to reveal anything. The prince was as restive as a man forced to sleep on a bed of thorns.

His second concern—his own future. Who can answer, in an instant, the question, what will happen now? The prince realized he was a prisoner. Osman and Ayesha in their compassion had ensured that he was spending his days in a well-appointed, well-aired chamber instead of being in prison. Servants and maids tended to him, his needs were met even before he could express them. However, there were still guards at the door; he was kept like a bird satiated with flavoured water in a gilded cage. Would he be released? What was the likelihood? Where were all his troops? In what state were they without their general?

His third concern—Ayesha. How had this maker of miracles, this embodiment of goodness, descended on this earth?

Jagatsingh had observed that Ayesha never rested, nor did she feel exhausted, or neglect her duty. She tended to the patient day and night. While recovering, he had seen her approach silently every morning on her graceful feet, like the sun at dawn, holding flowers in her hand. She never left the chamber before the hour for her ablutions and related tasks. She would return in a few minutes, rising thereafter from his bedside only if it was absolutely necessary. Until her mother, the Begum, dispatched an attendant to summon her, she would not pause for an instant in her nursing of the sick.

Is there anyone who has not had to take to bed out of an ailment? But only the one who has received the care of a bewitching woman by his bedside knows that even ailments can provide pleasure.

Do you wish to experience Jagatsingh's condition yourself, dear reader? In your imagination, lie on his bed, feel the agony of his wounds in your body; recollect that you are held captive by your enemies; and then conjure up in your mind the balmy, luxurious, pleasant chamber. As you lie on this bed, looking at the door, your expression suddenly becomes joyful; the one who treats you like a brother in your enemy's mansion approaches. She is, moreover, a woman, a young woman, a lotus in full bloom! Still lying on your bed, you gaze at her—consider her appearance. She is slightly—only slightly—on the taller side, an embodiment of the supreme goddess, the very symbol of the empress of the natural order of life. Look at her delicate bearing. You are thinking of the elephant's gait? You are mistaken—think of the swan's instead. Look at those steps fall, one after another—it is the rhythm of musical harmony, the rhythm of a musical instrument; the rhythm of those footsteps resonates in your heart. Look at those flowers in her hand; have you ever known flowers to lose their lustre because of the glow from the hand holding them? Have you ever seen the necklace lose its glitter because of the neck it adorns? Why do your eyes not shut for even an instant? Have you observed how beautiful the turn of her neck is? Have you regarded how her ebony hair cascades down to her ivory nape? Have you seen how her earrings sway on either side? Have you noted the subtle—so subtle—tilt of her head? It is evident only because of her height. Why do you look so intently at her? What will Ayesha think?

As long as Jagatsingh's ailment needed attention, Ayesha remained engaged in this manner every day. Then, as the prince's illness abated gradually, Ayesha's visits also became less frequent. When Jagatsingh had recovered completely, her visitations ceased almost entirely—she would appear but once or twice a day. Just as the winter sun withdraws gradually from the chilled person's body as the day draws to a close, Ayesha, too, withdrew from Jagatsingh gradually during his period of recovery.

One afternoon Jagatsingh was standing at the window of his chamber, observing the people outside the fort, despondently comparing his own condition to theirs. They were unrestricted, free to go wherever they wanted to. Several were gathered in a circle. The prince turned his eyes towards them. He realized that the crowd was partaking of some entertainment, listening closely to someone. The prince could not see who was in their midst but his curiosity was piqued. It was finally satisfied when some members of the audience left, and he saw an individual reading aloud from some sheets that appeared to be part of a manuscript. The prince was amused by the orator's appearance. He could be called a human, just as he could also be called a medium-sized palm tree struck by lightning. He resembled the tree in both length and girth; but no palm tree is ever laden with the weight of a nose of such dimensions. In form and appearance they were identical; the prince gazed in surprise at the movements of the orator's head and hands as he read. Just then, Osman appeared in the chamber.

After they had greeted one another, Osman said, 'What were you looking at so distractedly from the window?'

'Simply a log of wood. You can see it too,' said Jagatsingh.

'Have you not seen him before, prince?' said Osman after a glance.

'I have not,' answered the prince.

'He is the good Brahmin from your fort. His conversation is most amusing; I remember seeing him at Fort Mandaran.'

The prince found his interest rising—from Fort Mandaran? Would this person be able to bring him some news of Tilottama, then?

'What is his name, sir?' he asked anxiously.

'His name is obscure, I cannot recollect it easily,' said Osman, racking his brain. 'Ganapat? No... Ganapat... Gajapat... could it be Gajapat?'

'Gajapat? That is not a local name, and yet... he seems Bengali?'

'Indeed he is. Bhattacharya. He has a title too, something to do with... scholarship...'

'They do not use that word in Bengali titles, sir. They call it vidya. Probably Vidyabhushan or perhaps it is Vidyabagish, then,' said Jagatsingh.

'Yes, you are right, it *is* Vidya something... Wait, what is the Bengali word for elephant?'

'Hasti.'

'Any other word?' asked Osman

'Kori, donti, baaron, naag, gaj...'

'Ah yes, now I remember; his name is Gajapati Vidya Diggaj.'

'Vidya Diggaj! Scholar supreme! What an impressive title! One befitting his name. I am very keen to converse with him.'

Osman Khan had been privy to Gajapati's conversations. Talking to him could do no harm, he surmised. 'Why not?' he said.

Repairing to the antechamber, they instructed the servant to summon Gajapati.

125

Chapter Nine

Diggaj's News

WHEN GAJAPATI DIGGAJ entered with the servant, the prince asked, 'Are you a Brahmin?'

Diggaj answered, joining his palms respectfully—

'So long as the gods reside at the Poles and the Ganga runs through the earth, verily the best part of the senseless world is the father-in-law's temple.'

Suppressing his laughter, Jagatsingh greeted him reverently. Raising his palm in benediction, Gajapati said, 'May Khoda Khan keep you safe, babuji.'

'I am not a Muslim, sir,' answered the prince, 'I am a Hindu.'

'Blasted Yavana wants to trick me,' Diggaj told himself. 'He must be up to something, why else would he have sent for me?' He said apprehensively, his face glum, 'I know who you are, Khan babuji; your charity sustains me, pray do not punish me, I am your servant.'

Jagatsingh realized this was going to be difficult. 'You are a Brahmin, sir,' he said, 'and I am a Rajput, please do not speak thus. Your name is Gajapati Vidya Diggaj?'

'Oh my,' Diggaj thought. 'He knows my name. What trouble does he plan to get me into?' Joining his palms again in supplication, he said, 'I beg of you, Sheikhji. I am a poor man. Spare me, please.'

Jagatsingh realized that the good Brahmin was so afraid that he would clearly not serve the prince's purpose. To change the subject, therefore, he said, 'What is that text in your hand?'

'This is Pir Manik's text.'

'A Brahmin holding a pir's text!' said Jagatsingh in amazement.

'Sir… I was a Brahmin once, sir, but I am not one any more.'

The prince was both astonished and irked. 'What? Were you not in residence at Fort Mandaran?'

'Disaster!' Diggaj thought. 'He has come to know I used to live in Virendrasingh's fort. He will do to me what he did to Virendrasingh.' Terrified, the good Brahmin burst into tears.

'What is this?' said the prince.

Wringing his hands, Diggaj said, 'I beg of you, Khan sir. Do not have me killed, sir. I am your servant, sir, your servant.'

'Have you gone mad?'

'No sir, I am your servant. Yours and yours alone.'

To calm the good Brahmin down, Jagatsingh was forced to say, 'You have nothing to fear, pray read from the text, I want to hear.'

The good Brahmin began to read in a sing-song voice. He looked like a young actor in a drama troupe who has just had his ears boxed by the director.

A little later the prince asked again, 'Why were you reading from Pir Manik's text even though you are a Brahmin?'

'I have converted to Islam,' said the good Brahmin, interrupting his sing-song recitation.

'What!' said the prince. 'When the Muslim gentlemen came to the fort, they told me, "We are going to make you desecrate your religion, Brahmin." They forced me to eat chicken palo.'

'What on earth is palo?'

'Rice cooked with ghee,' said Diggaj.

The Rajput realized what he was referring to. 'Continue,' he said.

'Then they said, "You are a Muslim now"; I have been a Muslim since then.'

'What has happened to the others?' the prince found an opportunity to ask.

'Many other Brahmins have been converted to Islam the same way.'

The prince turned to look at Osman. Realizing his implicit censure, Osman said, 'What harm has been done, prince? The Muslims believe that Mohammad's is the only true religion; whether by force or by guile, there is nothing unethical about furthering the cause of the one true religion—on the contrary, it is right to do so.'

'Vidya Diggaj, sir,' said the prince without answering.

'The name is Sheikh Diggaj now, sir.'

'Very well. Do you not have news of anyone else from the fort, Sheikhji?'

Fathoming the prince's intent, Osman became worried. 'Swami Abhiram has escaped,' said Diggaj.

The prince realized that unless he asked the foolish man directly he would not get an answer. 'What has happened to Virendrasingh?' he asked.

'Nawab Katlu Khan has had him executed,' the good Brahmin replied.

Blood rushed to the prince's face. 'What? Is the good Brahmin imagining things?' he asked Osman.

'The Nawab sentenced him to death after pronouncing him guilty of treason in a trial,' Osman replied gravely.

Fire began to rage in the prince's eyes.

'May I ask another question,' he asked Osman. 'Was it done with your consent?'

'Against my counsel,' answered Osman.

The prince was silent for a long time. Considering it a good time to dismiss the good Brahmin, Osman told him, 'You may leave now.'

As the good Brahmin rose to his feet, about to depart, the prince restrained him by taking hold of his arm. 'One more question,' he said. 'Where is Bimala?'

The good Brahmin sighed, wept a little too. 'Bimala is now the Nawab's concubine,' he said.

'Can this be true?' The prince's eyes threw darts of lightning at Osman.

'What are you doing here still?' Osman told the good Brahmin without replying. 'Go!'

The prince held on even more firmly to his arm, and stopped him from leaveing. 'Stay another moment, just one more question.' His eyes were now bloodshot with flaming passions. 'What of Tilottama?'

'Tilottama has also become the Nawab's concubine,' answered the good Brahmin. 'They are living happily with their retinue of maids and servants.'

The prince flung the good Brahmin's arm away; he barely saved himself from falling.

'I am but a general,' Osman murmured, embarrassed.

'You are a demon's general,' the prince responded.

Chapter Ten

The Immersion

NEEDLESS TO SAY, sleep did not visit Jagatsingh that night. He felt as though he were lying on a bed of fire, his heart inflamed. Where once he would have considered the world void of meaning were Tilottama to be dead, now it was a matter of regret that the selfsame Tilottama had not given up her life.

What? Why was Tilottama not dead? Was her tender young body, enveloped in that soft, magical light, which Jagatsingh could always see in his mind's eye no matter which way he looked, now to be reduced to ashes on a funeral pyre? Was there not to remain a single memory of her body on this infinite earth? Whenever these thoughts assailed his mind, Jagatsingh's eyes streamed with unrestrained tears; but as soon as he was struck by the memory of the villain Katlu Khan's chamber of pleasure, as soon as he imagined her tender body encircled by the arms of the depraved Pathan, his heart was aflame again.

Tilottama was the goddess ensconced in the temple of his heart.

And the same Tilottama was now in the Pathan's chambers!

The same Tilottama was Katlu Khan's concubine.

Could a Rajput worship such a deity any more?

Was it worthy of a member of the Rajput clan to hesitate in removing such a deity from her pedestal with his own hands?

To evict the goddess established in Jagatsingh's heart would also rend apart the heart itself. How would he purge his memory of that enchanting woman forever? Was it even possible? As long as his faculties remained intact, as long as his flesh-and-blood body survived, she would reign as the queen of his heart.

These singular notions wreaked havoc on not just the prince's peace of mind, but also his intellect. His control over his memory loosened, even when the night had ended, he sat clutching his spinning head in his hands, all cogency of thought lost.

Locked in one position, Jagatsingh's body began to ache. He felt as if he were racked by fever, so intense was his agony. He rose and stood by the window.

A soothing summer breeze played upon his forehead. The night was pitch dark, the sky completely overcast. The constellations were concealed from view, with only a star faintly visible now and then behind the shroud of a moving cloud. The trees in the distance had merged with one another, standing beneath the sky like a wall of darkness, from nearer trees, rows of fireflies twinkled like the dust of diamonds; closer still, the sky and the trees were reflected indistinctly in a deep pool of water.

The touch of the soothing night breeze, borne by the clouds, alleviated his fever somewhat. He remained by the window, resting against it, his head in his hand. Exhausted by sleeplessness, he was granted a respite by the current of air. His mind wandered. The sharp pain of the knife in his heart was replaced by the dull ache of despondency. It is agonizing to abandon hope; but once dejection has rooted itself, the suffering is not as acute. A blow from a weapon is similarly painful, the ache from the wound that follows is constant, it is true, but not as extreme. Jagatsingh now endured the lesser agony of hopelessness. Gazing upon the starless black sky, he reflected with tears in his eyes that the firmament of his own heart had, too, become starless and black. His past came back to him gently along the lanes of his memories; his childhood, the diversions of adolescence, he recollected all of it. Jagatsingh immersed himself in his memories, becoming increasingly distracted. Gradually his body cooled, fatigue robbed him of wakefulness, leaning on the window, Jagatsingh fell into a slumber. The prince dreamt as he slept, his dreams tormented him. A frown creased his forehead, his face contorted in suffering, his lips quivered violently, perspiration covered his brow, he tightened his fists. Awaking with a start, he fretfully paced up and down the room. Who knows how long he endured this suffering. When the morning sun lit up the bulwarks of the fort, Jagatsingh was asleep on the floor, sans bed, sans pillow.

Osman arrived and woke him. When the prince was fully awake, Osman handed him a letter. The prince took it without a word. Osman realized that he was not quite himself. Aware that meaningful conversation would not be possible, he said, 'I will not ask why you chose to sleep on the floor. I have vowed to the sender of this letter that I would give her missive to you; the reason I have not done so all this time has ceased to be material since you have become aware of all that has passed. I am leaving the letter with you, pray read it at your leisure. I shall return in the afternoon. Should you wish to send a reply, I will give it to the sender on your behalf.'

Once he had regained possession of himself, Jagatsingh sat down to read Bimala's missive. When he had finished, he lit a fire and flung the letter into the flames, gazing at it as it burnt. When the letter had been burnt completely to ashes, the prince said to himself, 'If I can hurl the relic of the past into the flames to destroy it, why can I not destroy my painful memories too?'

He completed his ritual morning ablutions. Then he began to pray reverently to the Almighty. 'My Lord! Do not forsake your servant. Bless me so that I can uphold the royal ethic, so that I can act as befits my clan. I shall dismiss the heathen's concubine from my mind. If that means the destruction of this body, so be it, for I shall have you. I have done what a human being can, now I shall do what a human being should. Look at me, my Lord! You are all-seeing, you can look deep into my heart, I am no longer a suitor for Tilottama's affections, I am no longer desirous of setting my eyes on her, it is only my memories that are constantly burning my soul. I have forsaken desire, O Lord, will the memory not be extinguished? That is all I beg of you for I cannot endure the agony of remembrance.'

The goddess in the temple of his heart was immersed.

What was Tilottama dreaming of then, lying on the floor? The solitary guiding star she had looked upon in the darkness would no longer show her the way. The storm snapped the fragile thread by which her life had been hanging, the raft on which she was crossing the waves capsized.

Chapter Eleven

Change of Residence

THAT AFTERNOON, OSMAN appeared before the prince as he had promised. 'Do you wish to send a reply, prince?' he asked.

The prince had already composed his reply, which he now handed over to Osman. Accepting it, Osman said, 'Do not be offended, our rules demand that when an occupant of the fort wishes to send a letter to someone, the guards may not dispatch it without perusing its contents.'

'You need not state the obvious,' declared the prince, somewhat disappointed. 'Pray open the letter and read it, send it to its recipient thereafter if you desire to.'

Osman opened the letter. All that was written in it was:

'I shall not forget your request, victim of fate. But if you are a pious wife, you shall cleanse yourself of disgrace by following your husband presently. Jagatsingh.'

'Your heart is made of stone, prince,' remarked Osman on reading the letter.

'No more than that of a Pathan,' responded the prince acerbically.

Osman turned red with rage. 'I believe no Pathan has been uncivil to you,' he said somewhat harshly.

The prince was both affronted and embarrassed. He said, 'No sir. It is not myself I speak of. You have been merciful to me in every respect, sparing me my life even after taking me prisoner. You have cured the slayer of your troops of a near-fatal ailment. You have offered a life of luxury to one who should be languishing in prison. What more can you possibly do? But I am entrapped in your web of civility; I cannot fathom the outcome of this pleasant existence. If I am a prisoner, let me be lodged in a prison cell, free from your shackles of kindness. But if I am not, why am I locked in this gilded cage?'

'Why do you long for distress, prince?' Answered Osman calmly. 'Ill fortune need not be wooed, she comes on her own.'

'A Rajput does not consider it ill fortune to forsake this comfortable bed of yours for the rocks inside a prison,' declared the prince proudly.

'If only a bed of rocks were the biggest misfortune that could befall you, what harm would that do?' Answered Osman.

Looking sharply at Osman, the prince said, 'If I cannot teach Katlu Khan the lesson he deserves to be taught, what harm can death itself do?'

'Careful, prince!' warned Osman. 'Pathans do not make empty threats.'

'If you are here to frighten me, general, consider your mission wasted,' said the prince laughing.

'We are too familiar with each other to indulge in empty words,' said Osman. 'I have come to you for a reason.'

'I am at your command,' said Jagatsingh in surprise.

'The proposal I am about to make has been sanctioned by Katlu Khan,' declared Osman.

J: Very well.

O: Listen closely. The war between the Rajputs and the Pathans is causing harm to both adversaries.

'Causing harm to the Pathans is the precise object of this war,' answered Jagatsingh.

'True,' acknowledged Osman, 'but I am sure you can conclude for yourself how high the chances of victory, barring total extermination of both sides, are for either of us. You have observed that the conquerors of Fort Mandaran are not quite lacking in force.'

'Certainly not in cunning,' Jagatsingh said smiling faintly.

'Be that as it may,' continued Osman, 'personal glory is not my objective. Pathans shall not be able to occupy Utkal in peace if they are at war all their lives with the Mughals. But nor will the Mughal emperor ever succeed in bringing the Pathans under his control. Do not interpret this as a sign of conceit. You are politically astute, after all— consider the enormous distance between Delhi and Utkal. Assume that the Emperor of Delhi succeeds in defeating the Pathans this time with the help of Mansingh's power; but how long will his standard fly in this land? As soon as King Mansingh withdraws with his army, the Emperor of Delhi will cede whatever right he had gained to Utkal. Akbar Shah had conquered Utkal earlier, but how long did his reign last? Even if victory were to be achieved this time, the same outcome shall ensue. The Pathans are not like the Bengalis—they will never submit to being ruled; not even if only one of them is left alive. I can state this with certainty. Why then allow the earth to be flooded with the blood of Rajputs and Pathans?'

'What do you propose?' asked Jagatsingh.

'I propose nothing. It is my lord who has suggested a truce.'

J: What kind of truce?

O: Let both sides accept some concessions. Nawab Katlu Khan is willing to relinquish the portions of Bengal that he has annexed by force. Let Akbar Shah also give up his claim to Utkal and return with his soldiers, and refrain from invasions in future. This will cause no harm to the Emperor—on the contrary, it will harm the Pathans; we are offering to relinquish what we have won with our effort. Akbar Shah is only giving up what he has not succeeded in conquering.

'Excellent,' said the prince after listening to this. 'But why bring these proposals to me? King Mansingh is the arbiter of alliances; dispatch a messenger to him.'

'A messenger had been sent to the king,' said Osman. 'Unfortunately someone has informed him that the Pathans have taken your life. Driven by rage and sorrow, the king refused to even entertain the thought of a truce. He refused to believe the messenger. But if you were to bear the proposal personally, he would agree.'

The prince scrutinized Osman and said, 'Pray be explicit. The king would be convinced that I am alive even if he were to see my handwriting. Why then are you asking me to go to him personally?'

O: King Mansingh is unaware of the situation here; he will learn the truth from you. Moreover, your request is more likely to succeed, in a manner that a letter cannot. Another pleasant outcome of the truce will be that you shall be free once more. Hence Nawab Katlu Khan has determined that you shall personally appeal for this truce.

J: I am not unwilling to appear in my father's presence.

O: I am pleased to hear that; but we have another stipulation. If you are unable to ensure a truce as indicated, you must promise to return to this fort.

J: What assurance do you have that I shall return just because I have promised?

'It is a certainty.' Osman smiled. 'Everyone knows a Rajput never breaks his word.'

Pleased, the prince said, 'I promise to return alone to the fort after meeting my father.'

O: If you agree to another condition, too, we shall be especially grateful. Promise that you shall endeavour to conclude the treaty on our terms if you get an audience with the king.

'I cannot make this promise, general,' said the prince. 'The Emperor of Delhi has engaged us to defeat the Pathans, and that is what I shall seek to accomplish. He has not engaged us to conclude a peace treaty, I shall not do it. Nor shall I make such an appeal.'

Osman's expression revealed both satisfaction and displeasure. 'You have answered like a true Rajput, but consider this—you have no other means to secure your freedom.'

J: What does the Emperor of Delhi care for my freedom? There are many more princes, too, among the Rajputs.

'Take my advice, prince, forsake this thought,' pleaded Osman in disappointment.

J: Why, sir?

O: I will not lie, prince. It is only because you can serve his purpose that the Nawab has kept you in comfort; if you decline, you will invite considerable trouble on yourself.

J : Threats again! Did I not request you to imprison me only a short while ago?

O: If the Nawab is satisfied only with incarceration, prince, consider it a blessing.

The prince arched his eyebrows. 'What does it matter if I too am executed like Virendrasingh?' he said. Angry sparks flew from his eyes.

'I shall take your leave,' said Osman. 'I have done my duty. A different messenger shall convey Katlu Khan's order to you.'

The messenger arrived in a short while. He was attired like a warrior belonging to a rank somewhat superior to that of the common soldier and was accompanied by four armed foot soldiers. 'What do you want?' the prince asked him.

'Your residence is being changed,' the warrior told him.

'I am ready, lead on,' said the prince, following him.

Chapter Twelve

Deceptive Appearance

GRAND CELEBRATIONS WERE at hand. It was Katlu Khan's birthday. Everyone was engaged in diversions, dance, games, food, drink, etcetera, in the day—and even more so at night. Evening had just deepened, the entire fort was illuminated. Soldiers, sentries, noblemen, servants, citizens, mendicants, drunkards, actors, danseuses, singers, songstresses, musicians, conjurors, flower sellers, perfume sellers, paan sellers, food vendors, artefact sellers all thronged the grounds. Wherever you went, there were only garlands of light, music, scented water, paan, flowers, fireworks, whores. It was largely the same story in the inner chambers too. The Nawab's pleasure palace was quieter, but also more luxurious. In every room lamps of silver, lamps of crystal, aromatic lamps showered soft beams of light. Fragrant flowers adorned vases, pillars, beds, seats, and ladies. The air could scarcely bear the weight of the scent of roses. Countless handmaidens—some dressed in gold, while others in blue, rust, green, pink or brick-red silk, each according to their taste—wandered about, brightening the lamplight with the gleam from their gold ornaments. The ladies whom they served were seated in their chambers, tending to their wardrobe for the evening with great attention. Tonight the Nawab would include everyone in the festivities in his palace of pleasure; there would be singing and dancing. Each of the women would have her desire met tonight. One ran her comb swifter through her hair in the hope of securing employment for her brother. Another let her hair loose upon her breasts and plotted on increasing her number of maids. One wanted to get her hands on property for her newborn, rubbing her cheeks to redden them, even drawing blood. Yet another, coveting ornaments like those recently acquired by some other concubine from the Nawab, drew deep lines of kohl under her eyes. Somewhere a maid accidentally trod on a virago's pajamas while trying to dress her, and received a slap for her troubles. Elsewhere, a maid mistakenly uprooted a few strands of a lady's hair, now weakened by her advancing years. At their sight the middle-aged owner of the locks wept loudly, her eyes streaming with tears.

Like a lily among wild flowers, like a peacock among birds, one of the beauties—her coiffure set already—was wandering from one chamber to another. Tonight no one was forbidden entry anywhere. The Almighty had bestowed every variety of beauty in the world upon this woman and Katlu Khan had bestowed every variety of ornament on her; yet her face bore not a trace of the haughtiness of beauty or the conceit of precious possessions. It held neither levity nor laughter. Her countenance was serene, grave; there was a deep suffering in her eyes.

Wandering thus within the palace, Bimala entered a beautifully decorated chamber, closing the door as soon as she had stepped over the threshold. Even on this festive night, only a faint light was lit in that chamber. At one end of the chamber was a bedstead, on which lay a figure, covered from head to toe in a sheet. 'I have come,' murmured Bimala, standing beside the bed.

Startled, the person who was lying on the bed uncovered her face. Recognizing Bimala, she cast aside the sheet covering her and sat up, without answering.

'I am here, Tilottama,' Bimala repeated.

Still Tilottama did not reply, only looking at Bimala intently.

140

Tilottama was no longer a young maiden numbed by bashfulness. At that moment, under the faint light, she looked as though she had aged ten years. Her frame was emaciated, her face gaunt. Her garments were plain and tattered. Her dishevelled hair was matted with dirt. There was not a hint of jewellery on her, only a few traces remained of the ornaments she was once adorned in.

'I had said I would come—and I have,' Bimala continued. 'Why do you not speak?'

'I have said all that I had to, what else is left to say?' Tilottama said.

Bimala realized from her tone that she had been weeping. Putting her hand on Tilottama's head and tilting her face upward, she saw it was drenched in tears. Tilottama's scarf felt damp under her fingers. The pillow on which she had laid her head was soaked, too. 'If you weep like this day and night, how long do you expect to survive?'

'What use is it to survive?' said Tilottama passionately. 'My regret is that I have survived all this time.'

Bimala did not reply. She began weeping too.

After some time, Bimala sighed deeply, and asked, 'And what of tonight?'

Glancing disapprovingly once more at Bimala's ornaments and finery, Tilottama said, 'What of tonight?'

'Do not be flippant, my girl,' said Bimala. 'Have you not come to know Katlu Khan well enough yet? The villain has excused us this far, partly because he has not had the convenience, and partly out of the desire to give us the opportunity to contain our grief. But our exemption ends tonight. Who knows how he will vent his fury if he does not see us at the festivities.'

'What fresh fury can he vent?' said Tilottama.

'Why give up all hope, Tilottama?' said Bimala, calming down. 'Our hearts still beat in our bodies, we still know our duty. As long as we are alive, we shall do our duty.'

'Then throw away all these ornaments, mother. I cannot stand you in this finery,' Tilottama responded.

'Do not scold me till you have seen all my finery, my girl,' said Bimala with a smile.

She extracted a sharp dagger hidden in her clothes; its pointed tip flashed like lightning in the glow of the lamp. Turning ashen, Tilottama said in surprise, 'Where did you get that?'

'Have you noticed the new maid in our chambers who came yesterday?' said Bimala.

T: I have. Aasmani is here.

B: I had Aasmani fetch this from Swami Abhiram.

Tilottama was silent; her heart trembled. A little later Bimala asked, 'Will you not give up this dress for tonight?'

'No,' said Tilottama.

B: Will you not come for the singing and the dancing?

T: No.

B: You will still not be spared.

Tilottama began to weep. 'Listen quietly now. I have made arrangements for your release.' Tilottama looked at her eagerly. Giving Osman's ring to Tilottama, Bimala said, 'Take this ring, and do not go to the dance chambers. The celebrations shall not be completed this side of midnight, I will be able to keep the Pathan at bay until then. He has discovered that you are my stepdaughter; I shall prevent him from exercising his desire for your company until then on the pretext that you cannot appear there in my presence. At midnight go to the door of the women's chambers, a man waiting for you there will display a ring identical to this one. You can go with him without any fear, and he will take you wherever you tell him to. Ask him to take you to Swami Abhiram's hut.'

Tilottama was thunderstruck; whether out of astonishment or joy, she could not speak for some time. Eventually she said, 'Tell me more. Who has given you this ring?'

'That is a long story; I shall recount it to you at leisure,' answered Bimala. 'For now, do as I told you, without hesitation.'

'What will happen to you? Will you escape through some other means?' asked Tilottama.

'Do not worry about me. I will make my exit another way and meet you again tomorrow morning,' Bimala assured Tilottama.

Tilottama did not realize that Bimala had blocked her own route of escape for her sake.

It had been a long time since Tilottama's face had showed any sign of joy; today, at long last she looked happy.

The sight filled Bimala's heart. 'Now let me go,' she said, her voice choking with emotion.

'I see you are in possession of all the news in the fort,' said Tilottama hesitantly. 'Where are all our family? Before you leave, tell me how they are faring.'

Bimala realized that even in her sea of despair, Tilottama's heart was renewing its relationship with Jagatsingh. She had received the prince's cruel letter, which had made not a mention of Tilottama. But telling her that would only add to Tilottama's agony—so Bimala made no reference to it. 'Jagatsingh is in this very fort,' she said. 'He is in good health.'

Tilottama was silent.

Wiping her eyes, Bimala left.

Chapter Thirteen

Displaying the Ring

AFTER BIMALA LEFT, Tilottama's thoughts—as she sat alone in her chamber—gave her cause for both joy and sorrow. She reminded herself again and again of the possibility of imminent release from the villain's cage. She was doubly joyous dwelling on the thought that it was Bimala, who loved her more than life itself, who had arranged it. But then she wondered, 'Even if I am freed, where should I go? There is no such thing as home any more.' Tilottama began to weep again. As these thoughts jostled in her, another one rose in her mind. 'Then the prince is well? Where is he? In what condition? Is he a prisoner?' Her eyes misted over. 'Ah, fate! The prince is a prisoner because of me. Even if I sacrificed my life for him, would that be recompense enough? What can I do for him?' Her thoughts continued. 'Is he in prison? What manner of prison is it? Is no one else allowed in? What does he think of in prison? Does he recall Tilottama? But of course he does. I am the cause of all his suffering. How he must condemn me!' And then she thought, 'What is this? Why am I thinking thus! Has he ever been known to disdain anyone? It is not that, my worry is, what if he has forgotten me, or what if he believes I have been installed in a Yavana residence, what if he no longer has room for me in his heart because of this.' But immediately, she mused, 'No, why would he think that; I am imprisoned in the fort just as he is, why then should he hate me? But if he still does, I shall explain and beg him to understand. Will he not understand? But of course he will. If he does not, I shall lay down my life in his presence. In the old days women were tested by fire, not in this fallen age, but so what, I shall immolate myself in front of him.' After that, she wondered, 'But when will I get an opportunity to be in his presence? How will he be freed? What purpose will my escape serve? Where did my stepmother Bimala get this ring? Can it not be used for his escape instead? Who will be at the gate to escort me? Can he not accomplish this task? Yes, I shall ask him, let us see what he says. Can I not meet him once at least?' And then her thoughts told her, 'But how can I request a meeting? And even if there is one, what shall I say? What can I possibly say that will heal my suffering?'

Tilottama could not stop thinking.

A serving maid entered the chamber. 'What time of night is it?' Tilottama asked her.

'It is past midnight,' the maid replied. Tilottama waited for her departure. After the maid had completed her tasks and left, Tilottama left her chamber with the ring given to her by Bimala. Her anxieties returned. Her legs were unsteady, her heart trembled, her face was pale; each time she took a step forward, she took another backward. Eventually she mustered sufficient courage to proceed to the door of the inner chambers.

The inmates, the Negro guards and all others were participating in the festivities; nobody appeared to notice her, although Tilottama could not help feeling that everyone was watching. Somehow she negotiated her way to the entrance to the inner chambers. The sentries had given themselves up to pleasure. Some were asleep, some awake but dead to the world, others only partially conscious. No one noticed her. Only one man stood at the door—he, too, was dressed like a sentry. 'Do you have the ring?' he asked Tilottama when he saw her.

Apprehensively, Tilottama showed him the ring that Bimala had given her. After examining it carefully, the man in the sentry's uniform showed the ring in his own hand to Tilotttama. 'Come with me,' he told her, 'do not worry.'

Tilottama accompanied the sentry nervously. Almost everywhere, the sentries were as inattentive as they had been at the entrance to the inner chambers. Tonight in particular, the doors had been thrown open, no one said anything. The sentry escorted Tilottama through several doors, chambers, and terraces. Eventually arriving at the gate leading out of the fort, he said, 'Where do you wish to go now? Instruct me so that I may obey.'

Tilottama was unable to recollect Bimala's directions. Her first thought was of Jagatsingh. She wanted to say, 'Take me where the prince is.' But timidity, her old enemy, attacked her once more. She could not utter the words. 'Where do you wish to go?' the sentry asked again.

Tilottama could not speak, she seemed to have lost control, and suddenly she felt tremors in her heart. She could not see anything, could not hear anything; she was not even aware of the words slipping out of her mouth. The only word that the sentry could make out, indistinctly, was 'Jagatsingh'.

'Jagatsingh is imprisoned at present,' he said, 'in a place which is beyond the reach of anyone. But come with me, for I have been ordered to take you wherever you wish.'

The sentry re-entered the fort. Without any awareness of what she was doing or where she was going, Tilottama turned, too, like a puppet on a string, following him the same way. Arriving at the entrance to the dungeons, the sentry realized that, unlike the guards everywhere else who had become careless after all their carousing, every guard here was alert at his station. 'Where has the prince been imprisoned?' he asked one of them. The guard pointed with his finger. 'Is the prisoner awake or asleep?' the bearer of the ring now asked the prison guard. After checking, the guard said, 'The prisoner responded to my question, he is awake.'

'Open the door to his cell, this lady will visit the prisoner,' said the bearer of the ring.

'What!' said the guard in astonishment. 'Do you not know I have no such order?'

The bearer of the ring showed Osman's coded ring to the sentry. Bowing, he immediately opened the door.

The prince was lying on a humble cot in his cell. Hearing the door being opened, he looked in that direction curiously. When she was near the door, Tilottama found herself unable to move any more. Her feet were rooted to the spot; she held on to the door frame to prevent herself from collapsing.

When he saw that Tilottama was reluctant to enter, the bearer of the ring said, 'But what is this? Why do you wait here?' Still Tilottama's feet refused to carry her into the chamber.

'If you do not wish to enter, let us return,' continued the sentry. 'This is no place to wait.'

Tilottama prepared to turn back. But her feet refused to carry her in that direction either. What should she do now? The sentry grew anxious. Lost in thought, Tilottama advanced without realizing it. She entered the cell.

As soon as she set eyes upon the prince inside, Tilottama froze again; she supported herself against the wall by the door, her head bowed.

At first, the prince did not recognize Tilottama. He was astonished at the sight of a woman here—the more so because she only stood by the wall, looking at the floor, without coming nearer. Rising from his cot, he approached the door and looked at her closely.

For a fleeting moment their eyes met. Tilottama's lowered hers towards the floor at once; but she leaned forward slightly, as though about to prostrate herself near the prince's feet.

The prince stepped back, and immediately Tilottama stiffened, as though under a magic spell. Her heart, which had bloomed for a moment, shrank again. The prince spoke, 'Virendrasingh's daughter?'

Tilottama felt as though an arrow had pierced her heart. 'Virendrasingh's daughter?' Was this how he would address her now? Had Jagatsingh forgotten Tilottama's name too? Both remained silent for a while. 'What is your reason for this visit?' the prince continued.

'What is your reason for this visit!' What manner of question was this! Tilottama's head reeled; the chamber, cot, lamp, walls…everything seemed to spin around her; she leaned her head against the wall for support.

The prince waited a long while for an answer; but who would answer him? When he realized that a response was unlikely, he said, 'You are suffering, go back, purge your memory of all that has happened.'

Tilottama remained under an illusion no longer, she collapsed on the floor like a creeper severed from a tree.

Chapter Fourteen

Obsession

JAGATSINGH SAW THAT Tilottama had no pulse. He fanned her with his garments, but seeing no sign of her regaining consciousness, he summoned the guard.

Tilottama's companion approached him. 'She swooned all of a sudden. Who has come with her? Tell them to come and tend to her.'

'I am the only one who has come with her,' said the guard.

'You!' said the prince in surprise.

'No one else has accompanied her,' said the guard.

'What is to be done then? Inform a maid.'

The guard left. Calling him back, the prince said, 'There will be trouble if you inform anyone else. Who in any case will sacrifice the revelries tonight to come and help her?'

'That is true,' said the guard. 'And whom will the guards allow entry into the prison, either? I do not have the courage to bring other people in here.'

'What shall we do then? We have only one recourse; send word immediately through a maid to the Nawab's daughter.'

The guard left swiftly to perform his bidding. The prince tried to tend to Tilottama as best he could. Who could tell what thoughts ran though his mind? Who knew whether there were tears in his eyes?

Alone in the dungeons, the prince remained thus absorbed with Tilottama. What would happen if word could not be sent to Ayesha, if Ayesha could not help?

Tilottama recovered consciousness gradually. At that moment Jagatsingh observed two women approaching with the guard through the open door, one of them behind a veil. Even from a distance, her proud form, stately walk, and graceful neck told the prince that Ayesha herself had arrived with her maid; and he immediately felt reassured.

When Ayesha and her maid arrived at the door, the sentry asked the ring-bearing guard, 'Must they be allowed to enter too?'

'That is your decision, not mine,' said the bearer of the ring.

'Very well!' said the sentry, and refused admission to the women.

At his refusal, Ayesha parted her veil, saying, 'Let me in, sentry. If it causes you any harm, you may blame me.'

The sentry did not know Ayesha. The maid told him surreptitiously who she was. The astonished sentry greeted her, saying with his palms joined in supplication, 'Pardon the poor man's error, you may go wherever you wish to.'

Ayesha entered the prison. She was not smiling though she appeared to be, it was only her natural expression. In her presence, the prison suddenly seemed transformed, a prison no longer.

Greeting the prince, Ayesha said, 'What is this, prince?'

What could the prince answer? Instead, he only pointed to Tilottama, lying on the floor.

'Who is she?' asked Ayesha, examining her.

'Virendrasingh's daughter,' answered the prince uncertainly.

Ayesha sat on the floor, cradling Tilottama in her arms. Others may have hesitated, thought twice; Ayesha simply gathered her up in her lap.

Whatever Ayesha did presented a delightful sight. She made every act look graceful. 'How beautiful,' both the prince and the maid thought, when she held Tilottama.

Ayesha had asked the maid to bring rosewater; she proceeded to sprinkle it on Tilottama, and gave her a few sips of it. The maid fanned her; Tilottama had already begun to regain consciousness before Ayesha arrived, and now her care brought her to her senses completely.

As soon as she looked around, she remembered the recent events; she was about to leave the chamber instantly, but the physical and mental toil of the night had exhausted her frail body. She could not leave; as soon as she recollected all that had happened her head started spinning again, forcing her to sit down. Taking her hand, Ayesha said, 'Why so anxious, my sister? You are very weak now, come to my chamber with me and rest. I shall ensure afterwards that you reach your destination.'

Tilottama did not reply.

Ayesha had already learnt from the sentry all he knew; fearing that Tilottama would suspect her, she said, 'Why do you doubt me? I may be the daughter of the enemy, but do not consider me a traitor. I will not reveal anything. Before the night is out, I will send you wherever you wish to go, the maid will accompany you. No one will divulge anything.'

Ayesha said this so gently that Tilottama did not retain the slightest suspicion any more. She did not have the strength to walk very far at that moment, nor could she stay by Jagatsingh's side, therefore she agreed. 'You cannot walk by yourself, lean on the maid,' said Ayesha.

Placing her hand on the maid's shoulder, Tilottama used this support to start walking slowly. Ayesha took her leave from the prince too; he looked at her, as though he wished to say something. Realizing this, Ayesha told her maid, 'Take her to my chambers and then return here to fetch me.'

The maid left with Tilottama.

'Such is our meeting, yours and mine,' said Jagatsingh to himself. Sighing solemnly, he remained silent, gazing at

Tilottama through the open doorway as long as she could be seen.

'Such is my meeting.' That was Tilottama's thought too. She did not look back as long as she was in Jagatsingh's view. When she did turn, he could no longer be seen.

'May I take my leave?' the bearer of the ring asked Tilottama.

She did not answer. 'Yes,' said the maid.

'Then return the coded ring that you have with you,' said the guard.

Tilottama returned the ring to the guard. He left.

Chapter Fifteen

Open Declaration

When Tilottama and the maid left the chamber, Ayesha sat down on the cot. There was no other place to sit, Jagatsingh stood near her.

Plucking a rose out of her hair, Ayesha began to pull its petals off. 'It appears you wish to say something to me, prince,' she said. 'If I may be of service in any manner, pray do not hesitate to ask; I shall be delighted to perform your bidding.'

'There is nothing in particular that I wish for at the present moment, my lady,' answered the prince. 'That is not the reason for my desire to seek your presence. What I want to say is that, considering my condition, I do not have any assurance of getting an audience with you again; possibly, this is our final meeting. The debt that I owe you can hardly be repaid with words. Nor do I have enough faith in destiny to believe I will get the opportunity to repay it with deeds. But my submission to you is, if ever it is possible, if it is a different day that dawns, do not hesitate to ask me for anything.'

So distressed and bleak did Jagatsingh sound that Ayesha, too, felt his pain. 'Why are you abandoning all hope?' she asked. 'Today's misfortunes need not continue tomorrow.'

'I have not abandoned all hope,' answered Jagatsingh, 'but I am not inclined to harbour any, either. I do not wish for anything in this life but its end. I do not desire to leave this prison. You do not know of all the sorrows in my heart, nor can I convey them to you.'

The melancholy in his voice astonished Ayesha, made her even more despondent. Her regal demeanour was forgotten, the distance disappeared; like a tender, affectionate woman, she took the prince's hand in her own soft hands, then discarded it immediately, and, looking up at his face, said, 'Why is there such deep sadness in your heart, prince? Do not consider me a stranger. If I may, allow me to ask…has Virendrasingh's daughter…'

The prince interrupted her before she could finish. 'Never mind all that. That dream is shattered.'

Ayesha was silent, and so was Jagatsingh. Both of them remained that way for a long time; Ayesha lowered her eyes.

Suddenly the prince was startled; a teardrop had fallen on his palm. Lowering his own eyes to look at Ayesha's face, he saw that she was weeping; tears were rolling down her glistening cheeks.

'What is this, Ayesha? You are weeping?' said the prince in astonishment.

Without answering, Ayesha shredded the rose in her hand. When the flower had been reduced to hundreds of tiny fragments, she said, 'I had never thought that this is how we would part, prince. I can endure much hardship, but I cannot leave you alone in prison, suffering such agonies. Come out with me, Jagatsingh! There are horses in the stable, return to your camp this very night.'

The prince could not have been more surprised had the supreme goddess herself arrived in person to grant him a boon. At first, he was unable to summon a response. 'Jagatsingh! Prince! Come with me,' Ayesha repeated.

After a long interval Jagatsingh said, 'Will you really release me from incarceration, Ayesha?'

'This instant,' said Ayesha.

J: Without your father's knowledge?

A: Do not worry about that, I shall inform him…after you have gone.

154

'Why will the sentry allow me out?'

Tearing off her necklace, Ayesha said, 'The sentry will be enticed by this reward.'

'If this is revealed you will be chastised by your father,' the prince repeated.

'What harm will that do?'

'I shall not go, Ayesha.'

Ayesha's face fell. 'Why?' she asked in disappointment.

J: I owe my life to you, I will never do something that can cause you pain.

'You are determined not to go?' Ayesha asked, her voice choking.

'No, go by yourself,' said the prince.

Ayesha lapsed into silence again. Once more tears began to roll down her face; she controlled them with great effort.

The prince was bewildered by Ayesha's silent weeping. 'Why do you weep, Ayesha?' he asked.

Ayesha did not reply. 'Honour my request, Ayesha,' the prince continued. 'If you can reveal the reason for your tears, pray do so to me. If laying down my life will stop these silent tears of yours, I shall do so. That I have accepted my incarceration cannot be the only reason for Ayesha to shed tears. There are many like me who suffer in your father's dungeons.'

Without responding to the prince, Ayesha swiftly wiped her tears on the scarf wound around her neck. Motionless for a few minutes, she said, 'I shall not weep anymore, prince.'

The prince was a trifle disappointed that his question had not yet been answered. Both of them remained as they were, their faces lowered.

Neither of them noticed that a shadow had fallen on the wall of the chamber. The person came up to them, standing still for a few moments, but still they did not notice him. The stranger then spoke in a voice trembling with rage, 'How admirable, princess!'

155

Raising their heads, they saw it was Osman.

Learning of the events of the night from his attendant, the bearer of the ring, Osman had been looking for Ayesha. Seeing him in his cell, the prince began to fear for Ayesha, lest she be admonished or humiliated by Osman or Katlu Khan. The possibility seemed strong, judging from the enraged tone in which Osman had mocked her. Ayesha understood what Osman was insinuating from his sarcastic tone. She blushed but betrayed no other sign of annoyance. 'What is admirable, Osman?' she asked calmly.

'It is admirable for the Nawab's daughter to be alone with the prisoner at night,' said Osman, in the same tone as he had spoken earlier. 'It is also admirable to gain unlawful entry into the prisoner's cell at night.'

This slur was unacceptable to Ayesha's pure soul. She responded, her eyes on Osman. He had never heard her speak so imperiously.

'It is my desire to visit the prisoner alone at night and converse with him. And whether it is an admirable or heinous act is not your concern.'

Osman was astonished, but even more furious. 'You shall hear directly from the Nawab tomorrow morning whether it is my concern or not.'

'When my father questions me, I shall answer him,' said Ayesha in the same tone. 'You need not concern yourself.'

'And what if I were to ask?' said Osman, continuing in his mocking tone.

Ayesha stood up. Once more she looked briefly, steadfastly at Osman; her large eyes seemed to become larger still. Her face, as beautiful as a flower, appeared to bloom a little more. She tilted her head with its crown of jet-black hair; her heart felt as though it were convulsing, like the mottled moss on ocean waves. She said slowly and clearly, 'If you were to ask, Osman, I would answer thus, the prisoner is my beloved!'

156

If lightning were to have struck inside the chamber at that instant, neither the Rajput nor the Pathan could have been more astonished. Someone seemed to have illuminated the darkness inside the prince's mind with a lamp. He now understood the significance of Ayesha's silent tears. Osman had already suspected this from certain signs, which was why he had confronted Ayesha in this manner, but he had never imagined that she would declare as much openly to him. He could not summon a reply.

'Listen closely, Osman, let me repeat myself,' Ayesha continued. 'This prisoner is my beloved—no one else but he shall find a place in my heart all my life. If the execution ground were to be bathed in his blood tomorrow...' Ayesha was trembling, 'still you shall find me establishing his image in the shrine of my heart and worshipping it till eternity. Even if I do not meet him ever again in my life after tonight, even if he were to be freed tomorrow and surround himself with a hundred other women, even if he were to denigrate me, I will still remain desirous of his love. Hear this too, do you know what I was saying to him while we were alone all this time? I was telling him that I could win the guards over with words or with wealth and that I could procure him a horse from my father's stables to escape to his father's camp. The prisoner refused to escape. Otherwise you would have seen not a sign of him.'

Ayesha wiped her tears again. After a short silence, she spoke in a different tone. 'I have caused you pain with all I have said, Osman, forgive me. You hold me in high regard, as I do you; what I have done is not right. But tonight you thought Ayesha a traitor. Whatever other sin Ayesha may commit, she is no liar. Ayesha can declare openly what she has done. I have told you in person—if need be, I shall say it in my father's presence tomorrow.'

Turning to Jagatsingh, she said, 'Forgive me too, prince. Had Osman not goaded me tonight, the agony of this broken heart would never have been revealed to you, no living creature would have learnt of it.'

The prince stood in silence, his soul burning in anguish. Osman did not speak, either. 'I shall say it again, Osman,' Ayesha continued. 'If I have erred, forgive me. I am your loving sister as I always was; do not let your former love for me ebb because I am your sister. Ill fate has led me into an ocean of agony, do not leave me to drown by denying me the love of a brother.'

With these words, the beautiful Ayesha left the chamber without waiting for her maid to return. Bewildered and speechless, Osman left for his own quarters.

Chapter Sixteen

Your Maid at Your Service

THAT NIGHT, THERE was a dance performance in Katlu Khan's palace of pleasures. Only his concubines were present for the occasion. Nor was there any audience except Katlu Khan himself. He was not like the Mughal emperors who spent their birthdays entertaining themselves in the company of courtiers. He preferred private enjoyment, and was desirous of physical gratification. That night he was surrounded by the women who occupied his pleasure chambers, immersed in their singing and dancing and laughter. No one other than the eunuchs who guarded the harem was allowed in. Some of the women were dancing, some singing, some playing on musical instruments; the rest were listening, Katlu Khan in their midst.

There was a profusion of substances designed to entice the senses. The instant you entered the chamber, a constant sprinkling of fragrant water provided a soothing sensation to your body. The eyes were blinded by the dazzle of silver, ivory, and crystal lampshades; flowers in unlimited quantities —here in the form of a garland, there as a bouquet, elsewhere as a mound, or woven into women's hair, or adorning their throats—emitted a gentler glow. Some wielded fans made of flowers, others were dressed in floral garments, yet others showered flower petals on the gathering. There was the scent of flowers, of sweet-smelling water, of aromatic lamps, of the bodies of perfumed courtesans—their fragrance pervaded the palace. There was the luminescence of the lamps, the lustre of the flowers, the glitter of the ornaments worn by the women; most of all, there was the brilliance of the frequent, seductive glances bestowed by clusters of enchantresses. Sweet, melodious harmonies rose skywards from musical instruments, mingled with clearer, captivating, female voices in song; the rhythm and cadence of the danseuses' feet, anklets tinkling, bewitched the gathering.

Behold, reader! There is the swan dancing amidst a bloom of lotuses, in the gently rippling breeze; she is surrounded by beautiful, happy faces. Look, look at her, that lovely lady in blue, whose attire is studded with gold. There on the other side. Have you observed how splendid is the beauty's forehead, the parting in her hair adorned with a diamond star? Calm, clean, capacious; had the Almighty indeed condemned the owner of a forehead such as this to a harem? Have you noticed how her floral garments complement that beauty with her complexion like beaten gold? Flowers were created for nothing but adorning the female form. Do you see that woman with her full, rosy lips, curled a little, behold how her complexion shines through her silken blue attire, like the beams of the full moon reflected in the blue ocean. Do you see how the pendants in her ear sway as the woman, her neck curving more beauteously than the swan's, smiles and speaks? Who are you, you with the luxuriant coils? Why have you allowed your ringlets to hang over your breasts? Are you demonstrating how the venomous adder winds itself around the lotus stem?

And who are you, O alluring woman, who is seated by Katlu Khan's side, pouring wine into his goblet of gold? Who are you for Katlu Khan to ignore everyone else and cast hungry looks at your full-bloomed body continuously? Who are you, whose unerring glances have penetrated Katlu Khan's heart? We are familiar with that devastating glance—you are Bimala. Why do you pour so much wine? Pour, then, pour even more, you have your dagger concealed inside your garments, have you not? But of course you do. How then can you smile so much? Katlu Khan is gazing upon you! What was that? One of your glances! And again! There, you have aroused the Yavana already drunk on the taste of wine. Is this the ruse with which you have eliminated the others and become the object of Katlu Khan's affections? And why not—for how bewitching is the smile, how provocative the posture, how suggestive the conversation, how inviting the glances! Again you pour! Beware, Katlu Khan. But what can Katlu Khan do. It is the glance that accompanies the goblet of wine! What is that sound? Who is singing? Is this a human voice, or an angel's? Bimala has joined her voice to those of the singers. Oh, what mastery of melody, of voice, of rhythm. How now, Katlu Khan? Where is your attention diverted? What do you stare at? With those smiling glances accompanying each beat, she is plunging an instrument sharper than a dagger into your heart—and all you can do is watch? Those glances alone can kill, and now they have been joined by music. Have you observed, too, the subtle movements of the head along with those glances? Have you seen how the jewels sway from her ears? Yes. Give me wine, more wine, oh what is this now. Bimala has risen to dance. How beautiful! Oh, her poses! Give me wine! Her body! Her form! Katlu Khan! Your Majesty! Steady now! Steady! Oh! Katlu Khan is on fire. My cup! Ah! Give me my cup. My love! And what is this? More smiles, more glances? Wine! Give me my wine!

Katlu Khan was intoxicated. 'Where are you, dearest?' he called out to Bimala.

'Your humble maid is at your service,' answered Bimala, placing an arm on his shoulder. Her other hand held her dagger—in an instant Katlu Khan pushed her away with a horrible scream and sank to the floor. Bimala had plunged her dagger into his chest, up to the hilt.

'Witch—she-devil,' screamed Katlu Khan.

161

'I am neither a witch, nor a she-devil, I am Virendrasingh's widow,' said Bimala before fleeing from the chamber.

Katlu Khan was fast losing his power of speech. Still, he screamed as loudly as he could. His wives screamed as loudly as they could. Bimala shrieked too as she ran; at a distance from the chamber, she heard conversation. She fled as quickly as possible. In an adjoining chamber, she discovered guards and eunuchs. 'What has happened?' they asked, hearing the screams and observing her frightened condition.

'Calamity has struck!' said the quick-witted Bimala. 'Go quickly, Mughals have infiltrated the chamber, they have probably assassinated the Nawab by now.'

The guards and eunuchs raced towards the chamber. Bimala, too, escaped as quickly as she could through the door of the inner chambers. Exhausted by the carousing, the sentry at the door was asleep, Bimala emerged without being challenged. It was the same everywhere, she kept running unimpeded. At the outer gate, however, the sentries were awake. 'Halt, who goes there?' asked one of them on seeing her.

By then there was a tumult in the chambers within, everyone running in that direction. 'What are you doing here?' said Bimala. 'Can you not hear the uproar?'

'Why is there an uproar?' asked the sentry.

'Calamity has struck within; there has been an assault on the Nawab.'

The sentries deserted the gate to run inside, Bimala went out unscathed.

When she had travelled a short distance, she observed a man standing beneath a tree. At first sight she recognized him as Swami Abhiram. As she approached him, he said, 'I was exceedingly anxious, what is all the uproar inside the fort?'

'I have avenged the agony of being widowed,' answered Bimala. 'Instead of talking here, let us go to your residence.

I will tell you all afterwards. I hope Tilottama is there already.'

'Tilottama is walking on ahead with Aasmani, we shall meet them shortly,' said Swami Abhiram.

With these words, they proceeded apace, arriving presently at Swami Abhiram's hut to discover that, by Ayesha's grace, Tilottama had arrived with Aasmani a little while earlier. Tilottama threw herself at Swami Abhiram's feet, weeping. 'God has willed your escape from the clutches of an evil man,' he told her, calming her down. 'Let us not tarry in this kingdom a moment longer. If the Yavanas discover us they will assuage their mourning for their ruler by slaying us. Let us leave this place this very night.'

Everyone accepted this advice.

Chapter Seventeen

The Final Moments

MOMENTS AFTER BIMALA's escape, a palace official ran to Jagatsingh's prison cell. 'The Nawab is on his deathbed, prince, he wishes to see you,' he announced.

'What!' exclaimed Jagatsingh.

'The enemy penetrated the inner chambers of the palace and escaped after attempting to assassinate the Nawab. He is not dead yet, but the end is near, please come with me at once, or else it will be too late,' elaborated the official.

'Why does he seek to meet me at this hour?' asked the prince.

'I cannot tell, I am no more than a messenger,' came the response.

The prince accompanied the messenger to the inner chambers. He discovered that the light of Katlu Khan's life was indeed about to be extinguished, darkness was not far away. He was surrounded by Osman, Ayesha, his young children, his wife, mistresses, maids, courtiers, and others. Loud sobbing could be heard, most of those present were in tears; the children were weeping uncomprehendingly. Ayesha sobbed in silence, tears streaming down her face, as she cradled her father's head in her lap. To Jagatsingh, she was a picture of stillness, of gravity, of immobility.

As soon as he entered, a courtier named Khwaja Issa led him by the hand to Katlu Khan. Raising his voice, as one does to speak to the deaf, he announced, 'Prince Jagatsingh is here.'

'I am your enemy, dying…withdraw…anger hatred…' murmured Katlu Khan faintly.

'I do so withdraw them,' said Jagatsingh, understanding what Katlu Khan was seeking.

'Beg you to… accept,' Katlu Khan continued as faintly.

'Accept what?' asked Jagatsingh.

'Children all…war…thirsty,' still Katlu Khan continued.

Ayesha poured a little fruit juice into his mouth.

'No need…war…peace…'

Katlu Khan fell silent. Jagatsingh did not offer a response. Katlu Khan looked at him expectantly. When he realized no reply was forthcoming, he spoke with great effort. 'Unwilling?'

'I agree to make a request for peace provided the Pathans accept the supremacy of the Emperor of Delhi,' said the prince.

'Utkal?' gasped Katlu Khan.

'If I am successful,' answered the prince, discerning the import of Katlu Khan's question, 'your descendants shall not be displaced from Utkal.'

The dying Katlu's expression brightened momentarily.

'You are…free…the Almighty…bless…' murmured the dying man. As Jagatsingh was about to leave, Ayesha lowered her face to say something to her father. Katlu Khan looked at Khwaja Issa, and then again at the retreating prince. 'He seems to have something more to tell you,' Khwaja Issa told the prince.

When the prince returned, Katlu Khan said, 'Ear.'

The prince came closer to the dying man, lowering his face to bring his ear close to Katlu's lips. 'Vir…' said Katlu Khan, even more indistinctly than earlier.

He continued after a pause, 'Virendrasingh… thirsty.'

Ayesha held the fruit juice to his lips once more.

'Virendrasingh's daughter.'

The prince seemed to have been stung by a scorpion. He recoiled stiffly as though struck by lightning. 'Fatherless... I am a sinner...oh so thirsty...' Katlu Khan went on.

Ayesha gave him repeated sips of fruit juice. But it was almost impossible now for him to speak. 'Agony...chaste... you must...' he gasped somehow.

'I must...what?' asked the prince. His voice sounded like a clap of thunder in Katlu Khan's ears. 'She is...pure...like my d...daughter. You must...oh!...so thirsty...I go now... Ayesha...'

He could speak no more. The effort to speak as much as he had, proved to be his undoing; exhausted, his head slumped to one side. His daughter's name on his lips, Nawab Katlu Khan died.

Chapter Eighteen

The Duel

AFTER RETURNING TO his father's camp, Jagatsingh kept his promise, concluding a peace treaty between the Mughals and the Pathans. Despite acknowledging supremacy of the Emperor of Delhi, the Pathans retained control over Utkal. Detailed accounts of the treaty have been provided by history—elaboration is unnecessary. After the treaty was signed, both sides occupied their positions for some time. In order to seal their new-found cordiality for one another, Prime Minister Khwaja Issa and General Osman left for King Mansingh's camp, accompanied by Katlu Khan's sons; their gifts of one hundred and fifty elephants and other rare and valuable objects gave Mansingh pleasure; the king, too, gave them a warm welcome and bade them farewell with gifts of royal garments.

Some time elapsed thus in completing the peace treaty and preparing to break camps.

Eventually, when it was time for the Rajput soldiers to depart for Patna, Jagatsingh went to the Pathans' fort one afternoon, accompanied by his entourage, to bid goodbye to Osman and the others. Since their meeting in his prison cell, Osman had not displayed any amicability towards the prince. That day, too, he took his leave after a cursory exchange of pleasantries.

Bidding Osman farewell with disappointment in his heart, Jagatsingh proceeded to say goodbye to Khwaja Issa.

After that, he decided to bid farewell to Ayesha, and sent word through a guard, telling him, 'Tell her, we have not met since the Nawab's passing away. I am leaving for Patna now, another meeting is extremely unlikely—therefore I wish to greet her before I go.'

Returning presently, the guard said, 'The Nawab's daughter has said she will not meet the prince, she begs his forgiveness.'

His disappointment mounting further, the prince left for his camp. At the entrance to the fort, he discovered Osman waiting for him.

The prince was about to leave after offering his greetings once more to Osman, but he followed Jagatsingh. 'Command me, general, and allow me to be gratified by obeying you,' the prince said.

'I have something I wish to discuss with you, but not in the presence of your entourage. Send them on their way, and accompany me alone,' said Osman.

Without hesitation, the prince ordered his retinue to proceed, and accompanied Osman alone on horseback. They travelled some distance and entered a dense wood. In its middle was situated the ruins of a palace—there were signs that an insurgent may have concealed himself here in the past. Tying their horses to a tree, Osman led the prince inside the ruined palace. It was desolate. There was a wide courtyard within; to one side was a grave of the kind used by Yavanas, though it held no corpse. On the other side was a funeral pyre, without a body on it.

'What is all this?' asked the prince on entering the courtyard.

'All this has been prepared at my behest,' answered Osman. 'If I die today, you, sir, shall inter me in this grave, no one will know; if you are the one who passes away, I will have your last rites performed on this pyre by a Brahmin, without a third person's knowledge.'

'What do you mean?' asked the prince in surprise.

'We are Pathans,' responded Osman. 'When we are aroused by passion, we do not stop to consider right or wrong; there cannot be two suitors for Ayesha in this world, one of us must die here in this place.'

The prince finally understood. 'What is your intention?' he asked distressed.

'You are armed, I challenge you to a duel,' said Osman. 'If you can, slay me and clear your path, else die at my hands and leave the way clear for me.'

Without giving Jagatsingh the chance to respond, Osman launched himself upon him with his sword. In self-defence, the prince drew his own blade from his scabbard and parried Osman's thrusts. Osman made repeated attempts, with all his might, to slay the prince; but Jagatsingh only defended himself, without launching a counter-attack. Since both of them were well versed in swordplay, the duel continued for a long time, with neither able to defeat the other. The prince was lacerated with wounds by the Yavana's sword; his body was bathed in blood. But since he had not delivered a single blow on Osman, the latter was unharmed. With the loss of blood making him weak, and realizing that this battle could only lead to his death, Jagatsingh said in distress, 'Stop, Osman, I accept defeat.'

'I did not know that Rajput generals are afraid to die,' said Osman with a laugh. 'Fight on. I shall slay you, but I shall not forgive you. I will never get Ayesha while you live.'

'I do not desire Ayesha,' said the prince.

'You do not desire Ayesha, but Ayesha desires you,' said Osman, his sword whirling. 'Fight on, you shall not be pardoned.'

Flinging his sword away, the prince said, 'I shall not fight. You came to my aid in my hour of need, I shall not fight you.'

Kicking the prince in anger, Osman said, 'This is how I make soldiers fight when they are afraid to.'

The prince could hold his patience no longer. Reclaiming in a swift move the sword that he had deposited on the ground, he leapt on the Yavana like a lion who has been bitten by a jackal. The Yavana was unable to resist this fearsome assault. The force of the prince's enormous frame flung Osman to the ground. Planting a foot on his chest, the prince flourished his sword, then placed its tip against Osman's throat. 'Had enough of battle?' he asked.

'Not while I live,' said Osman.

'I could claim your life this instant,' said the prince.

'Do—otherwise, an enemy who desires to kill you will remain alive.'

'Let him, a Rajput does not fear such enemies; I would have taken your life, but because you saved mine, I shall save yours.'

Pinning Osman's arms to the ground with his feet, he disarmed the Pathan of all his weapons. Freeing him, he said, 'Now go home safely. You kicked a Rajput, hence I was compelled to do this to you, or else Rajputs are not so ungrateful as to lay their hands on their benefactors.'

When he was freed, Osman set off for the fort on horseback without a single word.

Drawing water from the well in the courtyard, the prince used his garments to wipe himself clean. Then he untied his horse from the tree and mounted it. Whereupon he discovered a letter tied to the reins with vines. Extracting the letter, he saw it was sealed with human hair, with the visible part bearing these words: 'Do not open this letter before two days. If you do, its purpose will be defeated.'

After some thought, the prince decided to comply with the writer's instructions. Tucking the letter into his armour, he spurred his horse and rode towards his camp.

The next day he received another letter delivered by a messenger. It had been sent by Ayesha. Its contents will be revealed in the following chapter.

Chapter Nineteen

A Letter from Ayesha

AYESHA HAD SAT down with a quill to compose a letter. Her expression was grave, composed; she was writing to Jagatsingh. She drew a sheet of paper to herself to begin. 'My heart,' she began, but scratched it out at once to write 'Prince' instead; replacing 'My heart' with 'Prince' forced a teardrop on to the paper. Tearing up the sheet, Ayesha began again. But no sooner had she written one or two lines than it was stained again by her tears. She tore up this letter too. Finally she succeeded in composing a letter untouched by her tears, but as she began to read it, tears welled up in her eyes again, clouding her vision. Somehow she succeeded in sealing the letter and handing it over to a messenger. The messenger left for the prince's camp with the letter. Ayesha lay down on her bed, sobbing.

Receiving the letter, Jagatsingh proceeded to read it.

'Prince,

'That I did not seek an audience with you was not because I lack faith in my own self-restraint. Do not mistake Ayesha for an impatient woman. There is a fire burning in Osman's heart, so I did not meet you, lest—who knows?—he be tormented by such a meeting. Nor did I have any hope that you would suffer were I not to meet you. As for my own distress—I have left it to the Almighty to decide on all my joys and sorrows. Had I been able to bid you farewell in person, I would have borne all the agony with ease. But now I must endure, stone-hearted, the anguish of not meeting you before you departed.

'Why, then, do I write this letter? It is only because of an appeal I have to make of you. If you have been told that I love you, force yourself to forget it. I was determined not to reveal it as long as I live, but it was God's will that it should be expressed; forget it now, I beseech you.

'I do not seek your affections. I have offered what I had to, I expect nothing in return. My love is so deeply entrenched that I shall be happy even if you do not offer your heart to me; but what use is it to speak of all that!

'You were unhappy when I saw you. If you ever find happiness, remember Ayesha and let her know. If you do not wish to, however, do not trouble yourself. But if you are ever tormented in your soul, will you remember her?

'That I am writing this letter to you, or if I write in the future, will displease many. I have done no wrong—do not, therefore, be troubled by their censure. Write whenever you wish to.

'You are going; you are leaving this land for now. These Pathans are not peaceful by nature. There is, therefore, considerable possibility of your return. But you shall not see me again. I have made this decision after a great deal of thought. A woman's heart is so hard to subdue that it is not wise to be too brave.

'I do envisage, however, meeting you one more time. If your wedding takes place in this region, inform me; I shall be present to preside over your marriage. I have gathered a few ornaments for your queen, if I get the opportunity, I shall adorn her in them with my own hands.

'I have one more appeal to make. When you receive news of Ayesha's death, visit this land, honour my request and accept what I have kept for you in the safe.

'What else can I say? There is so much I wish to, but it is unnecessary. May the Almighty ensure your happiness. Feel no regret when you think of Ayesha.'

When he had finished reading, Jagatsingh paced up and down in his tent for a long time, holding the letter. Then he suddenly composed a reply with quick strokes of his quill, and haned it to the messenger:

'You are a jewel among women, Ayesha. The Lord seems to desire nothing but pain for people's hearts. I am unable to reply to your letter, which has made me exceedingly unhappy. I cannot at this hour send the reply that I wish to. Forget me not. If I am still alive, I shall reply a year from now.'

The messenger bore the reply back to Ayesha.

Chapter Twenty

The Dying Lamp

Since Tilottama had bade Ayesha farewell and left with Aasmani, no one had heard anything about her. Nothing, too, was known of the whereabouts of Bimala, Aasmani or Swami Abhirama. After the peace treaty had been signed, the Mughals and the Pathans apprised themselves of the unheard-of misfortunes that had befallen Virendrasingh and his followers.Both sides agreed to find Virendrasingh's wife and daughter and reinstate them in Fort Mandaran. Accordingly, Osman, Khwaja Issa, Mansingh, and others instituted a thorough search for them; but none of them succeeded in obtaining any other information beyond Tilottama's departure. Eventually, a disheartened Mansingh installed a faithful retainer in Fort Mandaran with the instruction: 'Stay here and continue the search for the dead chieftain's wife and daughter; if you find them, reinstate them here in the fort and come to me, I shall reward you and give you another fief of your own.'

With this decision, Mansingh prepared to leave for Patna.

Whether what Katlu Khan had told Jagatsingh during his dying moments had wrought any change in the prince remained unknown. He did subject himself to considerable expense and physical effort for the search. Was it born of memories of the past? Or was it for the same reasons drove Mansingh and the others? Perhaps it was a result of a rekindling of his love. No one knew—but whatever be the reason, his endeavour was in vain.

Mansingh's soldiers proceeded to dismantle their camp —there would be a march on the morrow. The time came to read the letter attached to the reins of Jagatsingh's horse. Curious, the prince opened it and read it. All it said was:

'If you fear your Maker, if you are afraid of the curse of the gods, come here alone as soon as you read this.

I, a Brahmin'

The prince was astounded. He wondered if it was the ploy of an enemy, undecided whether to go. But the Rajput feared nothing other than the curse of the Brahmin—so he decided to respond to the summons. Accordingly he instructed his followers not to wait for him; they could advance on their own without harm, he would join them subsequently in Bardhaman or Rajmahal. With these orders, Jagatsingh set forth alone for the wood.

Arriving at the ruined palace, the prince tied his horse to the tree as before. Casting his eyes about, he could see no one. He proceeded to enter the palace. As before, he observed the grave to one side, the funeral pyre on the other. A Brahmin sat on the wood heaped on the pyre, his face lowered, weeping.

'Have you summoned me here, sir?' the prince asked.

When the Brahmin raised his eyes, the prince discovered on enquiring after his identity that he was none other than Swami Abhiram.

The prince felt surprised, joyful, and curious simultaneously. Offering respectful greetings, he said eagerly, 'How anxiously I have sought your audience all this time. But why are you in this place?'

Wiping his eyes, Swami Abhiram said, 'This is where I reside at present.'

Barely had he answered, then the prince plied him with more questions. 'Why did you wish to see me? And why do you weep?'

'The reason for my tears is also the reason for summoning you. Tilottama's death is near.'

Slowly, gently, one limb at a time, the warrior slumped to the ground. He recollected everything; each memory seemed to twist a knife sharply in a wound within him. The first encounter at the shrine of Shiva; the vow to meet again in the presence of the deity; their passionate tears in their first private meeting in the chamber; the events of that dreadful night; Tilottama's face as she lay unconscious; her torment in the prison of the Yavanas; his own brutal behaviour during his incarceration; and then death here in this wilderness—all these thoughts assailed the prince's heart like a whirlwind. The earlier flames flared a hundredfold.

The prince sat in silence for a long time. 'Since the day Bimala had avenged her widowhood by slaying the Yavana, I have been travelling incognito with my daughter and granddaughter, hiding from them—since then Tilottama has been afflicted by her sickness. You know its cause.'

Jagatsingh felt his heart being torn asunder.

'I have treated her in different ways in different places. I have studied the medical sciences in my youth, I have treated numerous maladies. I know of many medicines that are unknown to others. But there is no treatment for the affliction that lies within the heart. Because this place is desolate, we have been living here now, in this secluded spot, for the past six or seven days. When you appeared here by a miraculous coincidence, I affixed the letter to the reins of your horse. I had cherished the desire that, even if I could not save her life, I would ensure one more meeting between you and her to soothe her soul in her final hours. That is why I have asked you to come. All hope of Tilottama's recovery was not lost when I wrote the letter, but I knew that unless there was some improvement within two days, the end would be upon us. What I had feared has since come true. There is no hope of Tilottama's survival. The lamp is about to go out.'

Swami Abhiram began to weep once more. Jagatsingh wept too.

'You must not appear before her suddenly,' Swami Abhiram continued. 'Who knows, in her condition she may not be able to survive the intensity of the joy of seeing you. I have already informed her that I have sent word to you, there is a possibility of your coming. Now I shall inform her you are here, after which you may meet her.'

The sage walked away towards the inner chambers of the ruined palace. Returning after some time, he said to the prince, 'Come with me.'

The prince accompanied the sage in the direction of the inner chambers. There he saw a single room that had remained intact, in it a broken, dilapidated bedstead, on which lay Tilottama—wasted away by her illness, and yet in possession of a beauty that was far from being extinguished. Even in this condition, she retained her soft grace; she was as enchanting as the morning star about to be extinguished. A widow sat close by, massaging her limbs; it was Bimala—her body unornamented, her clothes threadbare, her appearance impoverished. The prince was unable to recognize her initially; how could he, age may have stood still for her once but she was now a woman of advanced years.

Tilottama had her eyes closed when the prince approached her and stood by her side. 'Tilottama,' Swami Abhiram addressed her. 'Prince Jagatsingh is here.'

Tilottama opened her eyes to gaze upon Jagatsingh; her glance was tender, full of affection, without the slightest sign of reproach. As soon as she had raised her eyes, Tilottama lowered them again, soon her eyes overflowed with tears. The prince could contain himself no longer; banishing his reserve, he sat at her feet, bathing them in silence with his own tears.

Chapter Twenty-one

The Dream Fulfilled

THE FATHERLESS, UNPROTECTED YOUNG WOMAN was on her sickbed and Jagatsingh was by her bedside constantly. Day passed, then the night, day came once more, passed once more, and it was night's turn again. The jewel of the Rajput clan sat by her dilapidated bedstead, attending to her needs and assisting the stricken, silent widow going about her duties tirelessly. He gazed upon the face of the suffering girl, wasted away by anxiety, waiting for the smile to reappear on her dew-soaked lotus-like face, waiting for her to bestow a glance upon him.

Where was his camp? Where the soldiers? The troops had broken camp and gone to Patna. Where was his retinue? They were awaiting their master by the Dwarakeshwar river. But where was their master? He was shedding tears on the tender flower bud wilting under an unforgiving sun, trying to revive it.

By and by, the tender flower bud was indeed revived. The most powerful magic ingredient in this world is affection. The strongest potion in illness is love. How else can a sick heart be mended?

Just as the dying lamp begins to smile again when oil is poured in drop by drop, so too are vines withered by summer rejuvenated by the advent of rains. With Jagatsingh by her side, Tilottama regained her life in the same manner day by day.

Gradually she became strong enough to sit up in her bed. In Bimala's absence they were able to open their hearts to each other. They said very many things, admitted many lapses, recounted the many unreasonable hopes that had been born in their hearts and died there too, talked of the many alluring dreams they had dreamt in slumber and in wakefulness. Tilottama told Jagatsingh of a dream she had had, while half-conscious, during her illness…

On a small hilltop replete with the beauty of the newly arrived spring, she and Jagatsingh appeared to be at play with flowers. Gathering the blossoms of spring, she threaded them into garlands, putting one around her own neck and one around Jagatsingh's, but caught by the sword slung at Jagatsingh's waist, the garland was severed. 'I shall not place a garland around your neck any more, I shall use it as shackles to bind your feet,' she said, weaving chains with the flowers. When she tried to put them on his feet, Jagatsingh stepped away. Tilottama ran in pursuit, Jagatsingh began to descend along the hillside swiftly. A narrow stream ran across their path, which Jagatsingh leapt across. Being a woman, Tilottama could not do the same, and with the hope of fording the stream where it would be at its narrowest, she ran downhill alongside it. But far from shrinking, the more she proceeded, the more the stream widened; soon it became a small river, then the small river widened to become a big river. Jagatsingh was no longer visible, the banks of the river became higher, uneven, she could barely move her feet. Moreover, large clumps of earth gave way beneath her feet, dropping into the river with a huge splash; there were vicious whirlpools in the water below, she dared not look. Tilottama tried to ascend the hillside again so that the river could not devour her. The path was uneven, her feet dragged; Tilottama began to sob loudly; suddenly the resurrected, and vengeful, figure of Katlu Khan appeared to block her way. The garland of flowers around her neck turned into a deadweight of iron chains. The chain of flowers slipped from her hands, falling on her feet and encircling her ankles in the form of iron chains; she was forced to halt suddenly. Capturing her neck in a vice-like grip, Katlu Khan whirled her around and flung her into the rapid currents of the river below.

Concluding her account, Tilottama said tearfully, 'This was not a mere dream, prince. The chain of flowers I had woven for you truly encircled my ankles in the form of iron chains. The garland of blossoms I had placed around your neck was indeed severed by your blade.'

Laughing, the prince placed the sword in his scabbard at Tilottama's feet. 'Here before you I shed my blade, Tilottama. Place your garland around my neck again, and I shall break my sword in two.'

When Tilottama did not respond, the prince said, 'I am not speaking in riddles, Tilottama.'

Tilottama lowered her face in bashfulness.

That evening, Swami Abhiram was reading a manuscript in a chamber by lamplight. Entering, the prince said respectfully, 'I have an appeal to make of you, sir. Tilottama is now capable of withstanding the strain of a journey, why then should she continue suffering in this decaying edifice? If tomorrow not be an inauspicious day, bring her to Fort Mandaran. And if you are not unwilling, pray gratify my desire by giving your granddaughter in marriage to the Amer dynasty.'

Dropping his manuscript on the floor, Swami Abhiram embraced the prince, blissfully unaware that he was standing on the sacred text.

When the prince was on his way to Swami Abhiram, discerning his intention, Bimala and Aasmani had followed him quietly. Waiting outside, they heard everything. When he re-emerged, the prince saw that Bimala had unexpectedly become her former self; she was laughing, pulling at Aasmani's hair and hitting her playfully. Ignoring the blows being rained on her, Aasmani was submitting to a test of her dancing skills. The prince walked past them quietly.

Chapter Twenty-two

Conclusion

FLOWERS BLOSSOMED. TRAVELLING to Fort Mandaran, Swami Abhiram ensured that his granddaughter entered into matrimony with Jagatsingh with great pomp and ceremony.

The prince had invited his friends and members of his retinue from Jahanabad to the festivities. Several of Tilottama's father's compatriots who were also invited joined the celebrations and plunged themselves into the revelries.

Jagatsingh had informed Ayesha too, as she had requested. She had arrived, accompanied by her younger brother—an adolescent—and escorted by numerous citizens.

Although she was a Yavana, Ayesha was given residence in the women's chambers of the fort by virtue of Jagatsingh and Tilottama's affection for her. The reader may imagine that a heartbroken Ayesha was unable to participate in the celebrations. In truth, it was not so. Aided by the ebullience of her own happy nature, Ayesha kept everyone in good spirits, dispensing her charm everywhere through her gentle smile, just like the swaying lotus in early autumnal bloom.

The wedding ceremonies were performed at night. Ayesha prepared to leave with her entourage, bidding farewell to Bimala with a smile. Bimala, who knew nothing, said, 'Now it will be our turn to be invited to your wedding, Your Highness.'

Taking leave of Bimala, Ayesha led Tilottama into a secluded chamber. Clasping her hand, she said, 'Now I shall go, my sister. I bless you with all my heart and soul, may you enjoy a life of eternal bliss.'

'When shall we meet again?' asked Tilottama.

'How can we expect to meet again?' asked Ayesha. Tilottama was disappointed. Both of them fell silent.

After an interval, Ayesha said, 'Whether we meet again or not, you will not forget Ayesha, will you?'

'If I forget Ayesha the prince will not keep my company,' said Tilottama smiling.

'That does not please me,' said Ayesha gravely. 'You must never talk about me to the prince. Promise that you shall not.'

Ayesha knew that her sacrifice would always remain a wound in Jagatsingh's heart. Even a reference to Ayesha could cause him to repent.

Tilottama promised. 'And yet do not forget me either,' said Ayesha. 'Do not discard the keepsake I shall give you.'

Summoning her maid, Ayesha gave her an order. As commanded, the maid fetched an ivory casket filled with jewels and ornaments. Dismissing her, Ayesha proceeded to adorn Tilottama in them with her own hands.

Although Tilottama was the daughter of a wealthy landowner, she was astonished by the exquisite craftsmanship and the extraordinary shine of the precious diamonds and other gems that the ornaments were studded with. As a matter of fact, Ayesha had given up all the ornaments inherited from her father to have this valuable set of jewellery crafted for Tilottama. As the bride began to extol the virtues of the trousseau, Ayesha said, 'There is no need to be full of praise, my sister. These ornaments are worth not a fraction of the value of the jewel that shall adorn your heart from now on.' Tilottama had not an inkling of the effort with which Ayesha contained her tears as she said this.

After she had dressed Tilottama in the ornaments, Ayesha took both her hands and gazed upon her face. 'This loving countenance does not suggest that my dearest one will experience even a single day's grief because of her,' she mused. 'Unless the Almighty decrees otherwise, I pray to Him that she gives him all the happiness he deserves till eternity.'

To Tilottama, she said, 'I am leaving now, Tilottama. Your husband is probably busy, I shall not distract him by bidding him farewell. May the Lord grant both of you a long life together. Wear the ornaments I have given you. And keep my... your prized jewel safe in your heart.'

Ayesha choked as she pronounced the words 'your prized jewel'. Tilottama saw her eyelashes trembling with unshed tears.

'Why do you weep?' asked Tilottama, moved. At this Ayesha began to cry, tears flowing down her cheeks.

Without another moment's delay, she left, climbing into her palanquin.

Night had not yet ended when she reached her own residence. Discarding her finery, she stood before the window. A soothing breeze blew in, a million stars glowed in a sky that was a softer indigo than the garments she had just shed; the leaves of the trees murmured in the darkness as they swayed in the gentle wind. An owl hooted softly, sonorously, atop the tower. Beneath the window, at the base of the fort, the overflowing moat silently took on the reflection of the sky.

Sitting by the window, Ayesha let her thoughts run. She removed one of the rings on her fingers—it held poison. 'I could drink this now and quench my thirst forever,' she mused. The very next moment, she reflected, 'But is this what God sent me to earth for? If I cannot withstand this pain, why was I born a woman? What will Jagatsingh say when he hears?'

She put the ring back on. Then, struck by a thought, she took it off again. 'No woman can withstand this temptation,' she reflected. 'It is wiser to get rid of it.'

Ayesha hurled the poisoned ring into the waters of the moat.

Translator's note

BANKIM CHANDRA CHATTOPADHYAY is believed to have written *Durgeshnandini*, his first Bengali novel, between 1862 and 1864. Despite alarming the orthodoxy, it was published to enthusiastic reviews in 1865 and went into thirteen editions. The first English translation was published as early as in 1880, indicating just how keenly Indians who could not read Bengali and, presumably, the English, wanted to read it.

Any novel that is being translated into English a hundred and thirty five years after its appearance naturally poses a question of how contemporary the translation should be in its choice of vocabulary, syntax, and structure. The written Bengali of that period was still a 'classical' one, not approximating the spoken language, but closer in tone to the high Bengali used in poetry. This is the language of *Durgeshnandini*. Since the novel abounds in dialogue, much of the speech is imbued with a formality of tone—often bordering, as a result, on the declamatory—except in very intimate exchanges.

Complicating things further is the setting of the novel—1592 Common Era, during the reign of the Mughal emperor Akbar. And although the theatre of the novel is Bengal, the characters are Mughals and Pathans, with a few locals thrown in, whose tongue was obviously far removed from the one in which the author makes them speak.

In *Durgeshnandini*, Bankim solved the problem of capturing a historical era by ignoring it—he simply used the accepted language of Bengali prose of his time. His writing was nevertheless replete with ornamentation, stylization, descriptions that are a tip of a hat to literary conventions of his era—more poetry than prose in spirit, more prose than poetry in letter. He was, after all, following in the slipstream of, among others, the epic verse writer Michael Madhusudhan Datta.

The challenge of translating *Durgeshnandini* is to retain this classical prose style yet not lose the narrative verve which is perhaps the novel's most exceptional feature. Bankim's own English novel, *Rajmohan's Wife*, serialized in 1864, may have offered a template. It was his first work of fiction, after which he wrote only in Bengali. However while *Rajmohan's Wife* is an accurate reflection of how Bankim actually used the English language, it cannot be used as a model for a translation of *Durgeshnandini* today. For the idiom is archaic, not merely historical, and would do no justice to the racy contemporaneity of the novel.

Taking a cue from Bankim's choice of what was to him a contemporary if literary idiom, this translation too does not attempt to recreate a historical English equivalent of the 'classical' Bengali of the original text. It uses, instead, a more universal form of the English language, without attempting to use Victorian English, which would place the novel in a society and geography far removed from both its setting and from India in 1865. Unlike in *Rajmohan's Wife*, for instance, the word thou has not been used in this translation.

The real relationship with the original, therefore, is allegiance to Bankim's voice, rhythm, and storytelling. Thus, the translation maintains the long, flowing sentences, the almost breathless tone of narration, the piling up of descriptive phrases, the sharpness of the verbal exchanges—all of it without deviating from the content as well as, one hopes, intent of each and every line.

186

As an example, consider this passage describing Bimala as she prepares to assassinate Katlu Khan. Bankim is, quite literally, in full flow here and this section continues in this vein for some length.

> Why do you pour so much wine? Pour, then, pour even more, you have your dagger concealed inside your garments, have you not? But of course you do. How then can you smile so much? Katlu Khan is gazing upon you! What was that? One of your glances! And again! There, you have further aroused the Yavana already drunk on the taste of wine. Is this the ruse with which you have eliminated the others to become the object of Katlu Khan's affections? And why not—for how bewitching is the smile, how provocative the posture, how suggestive the conversation, how inviting the glances! Again you pour! Beware, Katlu Khan.

Bankim was nothing if not a crafty master of the language, moving effortlessly between emotion, introspection, action and comedy in the course of his narration and yet keeping the pace of his storytelling relentless. This translation has attempted to preserve each of the individual registers. Here, for example, is an exchange between Gajapati Vidya Diggaj, the one comic character in the novel, and the maid Aasmani who he tries, unsuccessfully, to woo.

> Aasmani entered as soon as he opened the door. It dawned on Diggaj that his beloved deserved a worthy welcome. Therefore, he intoned, his arm upraised, 'I bow in reverence to you, o goddess.'

> 'And where did you discover such juicy poetry?' enquired Aasmani.

> D: I composed it today just for you.

> A: Not for nothing have I dubbed you the king of love.

The intensity of the dramatic moments, the twists and turns

in the plot, the graphic descriptions of battle, death and assassination are all conveyed in the original through precise detail, enhanced by similes and metaphors. The details remain in all their exactness; when metaphors and similes could not be transferred to English directly, they have been recrafted to sit easily in the language of the translation.

Finally to the title which has arisen out of a compromise. *Durgeshnandini* literally means the daughter (nandini) of the lord of the fort (durgesh). Perhaps the most appropriate English translation of this would have been *The Castellan's Daughter*, the word 'castellan' like 'durgesh' conflating the stature of the man with the property he owns. However 'castellan' feels too unused a word for today and thus the translation of 'durgesh' could retain only one of its meanings—that of a nobleman. Chieftain seemed the best word in this context as it seemed to imply the feudal world of Bengal and indicate Virendrasingh's position most accurately.

This translation owes a special debt to Professor Shirshendu Chakrabarti who ensured that it has not strayed from the original in meaning and interpretation. The result, it is hoped, would be pleasing to Bankim Chandra Chattopadhyay were he to read *The Chieftain's Daughter* today.

Rajmohan's Wife
Bankim Chandra Chattopadhyay

The beautiful and passionate Matangini, married to a villainous man and in love with her sister's husband, represents the vitality of women who remain strong in the face of brutality and the confining expectations of middle-class society. Bankim Chandra's vivid descriptions of the routine of Bengali households provide a revealing portrait of life in the nineteenth century.

Penguin Classics/PB

Chandimangal
Kavikankan Mukundaram Chakravarti

Translated by Edward Yazijian

A seamless translation of the greatest mangal kavya written in Bengali. The *Chandimangal* of Kavikankan Mukundaram Chakravarti is an exemplary work of epic scale that recounts the story of the Goddess Chandi's constant battle to establish her cult among humans. Through the three books of the kavya—The Book of the Gods, The Book of the Hunter and The Book of the Merchant—we are introduced to Chandi in all her manifestations, from the benevolent to the wrathful, from Abhaya to Chamunda. Mukundaram's captivating tales and vivid imagery bring together the enchanting world of the gods with the more challenging world of the mortals while critiquing sixteenth-century Bengali society.

In his exquisite rendering of the *Chandimangal*, Edward Yazijian manages to capture not only the performative and humorous but also the reverent aspects of the text.

Penguin Classics/PB

READ MORE IN PENGUIN CLASSICS

The Poem of the Killing of Meghnad:
Meghnādbadh kābya

Michael Madhusudan Dutt

Translated by William Radice

An epic in blank verse, *The Poem of the Killing of Meghnad* has Indrajit (Meghnad), Ravan's warrior son who is slain by Lakshman in the Ramayana, as its protagonist. But the manner in which Meghnad is killed by Lakshman—in a temple, where he has come unarmed to conduct a puja—is a departure from the Kshatriya warrior-code. This is the most subversive and original feature of Madhusudan's epic, and a daring way of turning Meghnad into a tragic hero.

This lyrical and vigorous translation by William Radice is accompanied by an extensive introduction, detailed footnotes and a comprehensive survey of Madhusudan's use of Indian and Western sources.

Penguin Classics/PB